DEAD GIRL BLUES

For PAUL VLACHOS

ISBN: 978-1-951939-63-2

Cover and Interior by QA Productions

A LAWRENCE BLOCK PRODUCTION

DEAD GIRL BLUES

LAWRENCE BLOCK

A MAN WALKS into a bar.

Isn't that the way it generally starts? Except there's something essentially urban about the word. A neighborhood bar, a dive bar, a downtown bar. A sleek hotel bar. An airport bar, to curb pre-flight jitters. A commuters' bar, conveniently located right across the street from the train station.

This was more what you'd call a roadhouse, maybe a mile outside of the city limits of Bakersfield. That's in California, or at least this one was. There may be other Bakersfields in other states.

I suppose you could look it up.

PICTURE A SQUAT building of concrete block, set on a one-acre lot. Plenty of room for parking. Plenty of neon, but I couldn't tell you what it said.

Country and Western music on the jukebox. Guys with Stetsons, women with big hair. Everybody wearing boots.

I walked in and my pulse quickened. No hat on my head, no boots on my feet, but I looked like I belonged. Still wearing my work clothes—dark navy pants, a matching shirt with a name embroidered in yellow script on the breast pocket.

A bad job of embroidering, so the name was hard to read,

but if you gave it some study you could see that it read *Buddy*. Not my name, not what anybody ever called me, except the occasional stranger who wanted me to move my car. The shirt had been left behind by the last man who'd had the job at the Sunoco station. I didn't mind. It fit me okay, and if I was going to pump your gas I'd as soon answer to *Buddy* as to my own name.

I went to the bar and ordered a beer. My usual order was Miller's, Miller's High Life, but it seems to me I didn't see it on the row of beer taps and ordered something else instead. Lone Star? Maybe.

Whatever it was, the bartender brought it. Took my money, put my change on the top of the bar. A few years since anybody thought about carding me. I was what, 25? 26?

I suppose I took a sip of beer. Then I looked around, and I saw her right away.

Only person there who stayed with me. I couldn't tell you if that bartender was old or young, fat or skinny. I couldn't even say for sure that it wasn't a barmaid. But I think it was probably a man. I think I'd have remembered otherwise.

But maybe not.

But the woman. Her hair, a medium brown with blond streaks, was the biggest thing about her. She was a little thing, with a slim figure. Wore a scoop-necked blouse and didn't fill it out all that much. Tight jeans. High-heeled boots that maybe got her clear up to five-three.

Drunk.

"Buy you another of those?"

She looked at my face, trying to figure out if she knew me. Then squinted at my pocket. "Hey, it's Buddy," she said.

Who am I and why am I telling you all this?

I am a man sitting at a laptop computer and tapping its keys, groping for the right words even as I work to keep my recollection in focus. I am the man in the present, observing and remembering, even as I am the man in the past, starring in my little drama.

Who, then? And why?

If I persist in this effort, and I'm by no means certain that I will, those questions will be answered in the telling.

I HAD NO business buying her a drink, and the bartender had no business selling her one. She was already well-oiled.

Well-oiled. Good term for it.

She drank her drink. Was it a glass of wine? A mixed drink? I couldn't tell you, any more than I could report on our conversation or say exactly how we got out of there. I'd parked at the farthest corner of the parking lot, and we were suddenly there and in the middle of an open-mouthed kiss.

She'd been drinking wine. Red wine. I remember now. Her mouth tasted of it.

I took hold of her butt, gave it a squeeze. Nice tight little ass. She reached for the front of my pants, held on to what she found there.

Then we were in the car, kissing again, and then I keyed the ignition and got out of the lot.

There was probably a lover's lane nearby, there always is, but I was too new to the area to know where to look for it. But I took this road and that road, turning whenever the road I came to was narrower and lonelier than the one I was on, and without knowing where the hell I was I managed to find a place to park. A grassy patch a few yards off the road, unlit except for what came down from the sky.

Was the moon full, or just a crescent? Was the sky clear enough to see it? You could look that up, too.

A lot I don't remember.

And a lot she wouldn't remember, because around the time I started driving, her eyes closed and she let the wine take her.

She stirred when I cut the ignition, but didn't wake up. I found a blanket in the trunk and spread it on the ground. It wasn't clean, but it had to be more comfortable than the bare ground.

Considerate of me. Always the gentleman.

Neither of us had bothered with seatbelts. I opened the door on her side, gripped her under her arms, and drew her out of the car. I'd walked her halfway to the blanket before she came awake, and the look she gave me made it clear that she couldn't remember ever laying eyes on me before.

She said, "Who the hell are you?"

"Buddy," I might have said, but I'm not sure I did. I'd never learned her name and she'd forgotten mine, and it wasn't my name in the first place. And I didn't care about either of our names. I just wanted to get her down on the blanket and fuck her.

Back in the roadhouse parking lot, I could have shoved her down on the blacktop and done her six ways and backwards, and she would have been fine with it. But that girl was gone, her place taken by a mean-mouthed bitch who wasn't having any.

What I thought: *Oh, good.*

I grabbed her right shoulder with my left hand, and I made a fist of my right hand, and I hit her as hard as I could, hit her in the stomach, hit her maybe three inches north of her belly button, high enough up to keep from hurting my hand on her oversize belt buckle. Hit her in the solar plexus, I guess you'd call it.

The breath went out of her and she doubled up. I thought she was about to puke, but she didn't, and I hit her again with my closed fist, this time on the temple.

Down and out.

THIS IS WHERE a person would say, *And then everything went black.* Or maybe red, like looking at the world through blood.

Or, *And that's the last thing I remember.*

Maybe they're telling the truth, maybe everything goes

black for them, maybe that's really the last thing they remember.

Different for me. You could say it's the first thing I remember. Pulling into the roadhouse lot, ordering the beer, buying her the drink—those are hazy memories, filled in with my knowledge of what must have happened.

But the minute the lights went out for her was the minute they came on for me.

Who are you and why am I telling you all this?

Now that's a subtly different question, isn't it? A knee-jerk response might be that I'm writing this for myself, to illuminate a life for the man who has lived it all these years, and of course that's true.

But not the whole truth, not the sole truth. If I were the only intended audience, why relate and explain that which I already know? Why show off with turns of language?

Why find oneself hesitating before uncomfortable revelations, only to steel oneself and write them down?

And so I envision you, Dear Reader, without devoting too much energy to wondering who you might be. And this seems appropriate, in fact, because there's every chance that what I'm writing will go forever unread. At the moment it's no more than a string of electronic impulses, stowed somewhere on the laptop's hard drive when I hit Save and stop for the day,

summoned up anew when next I find the file again and open
it.

At the end of any session—or even in the middle, even right
now if I make the choice—I have the option of dragging the file
into the trash and sending it off to Pixel Heaven. But of course
if I understand the technology correctly, Omar's observation
about the writing of the moving finger applies as well to anything one composes on a computer. "Nor all thy tears wash out
a word of it . . ." It's ineradicable.

Still, I could remove the hard drive and take a hammer to
it. I could chuck the whole laptop in the river.

But assuming I don't, and assuming I finish this and resign
myself to its being read, who'll be my reader? I don't really
know that. Someone in authority? Someone who knows me,
even cares about me? Someone I care about?

And, again, why am I telling you all this?

Perhaps we'll answer that together, you and I.

SHE WASN'T UNCONSCIOUS for long. By the time I'd posi-
tioned her on the blanket and got her blouse unbuttoned, her
eyes were open and she was looking at me. She was angry and
she was terrified, in about equal parts.

I was lying on top of her, and I was rock-hard, the blood
pounding in my ears. I was trying to get her jeans down over
her hips and she kept twisting, trying to get away from me,
and this was at once exciting and infuriating.

And I wanted to fuck her, and I would, but what I really wanted was to kill her. More than anything else, I wanted to kill her.

I got my hands around her throat.

Now her eyes went all the way wide. It seems to me they were blue, and they might have been, but I doubt there was enough light to tell.

She knew what was coming. She tried to cry out but she couldn't, she couldn't make a sound, and I lay full length on top of her and felt her little body trying to move beneath me, and my hands tightened and I squeezed her throat with every bit of strength I had, and I watched her face throughout.

And I got to see the light go out of her eyes.

GOD, WHAT A feeling!

It was like an orgasm of the mind. It was that feeling like when you come, but not in the genitals. I was still hard as granite, I was still desperate to penetrate her and empty myself into her, but in my mind I already felt something close to pure ecstasy.

And now she was mine to use as I wanted. I yanked the boots off her feet. I got her out of her jeans, peeled her panties down and off, got rid of her blouse and bra.

Sweet little tits. A flat stomach, and I dug my fingers into her solar plexus, where I'd struck her, but she was past feeling it.

Past feeling anything.

I forced my way inside of her and I fucked her, and she couldn't have been hotter or more delicious if she'd been alive. No need to control her now, no need to keep her from crying out. No need to care what she thought of me.

All I had to do was use her body to pleasure myself.

IT'S NOT HARD to remember. In fact I probably remember it too well. I've gone over and over it in my mind, letting it play on the screen of my memory like a favorite movie.

I do this not because I forget how it ends. I do it because the memory, like the occasion itself, is richly exciting. The past incident has become a present fantasy, still eliciting a sexual response, and like any fantasy one allows it to change form over time. One tries to improve it

Perhaps she cries out and begs. Perhaps, in an effort to save herself, she volunteers to provide oral sex; she's good at it and one hesitates to make her stop, but it's just so much better to wring her neck.

And so on.

But to trim the trimmings and hew to the truth, I fucked her dead body until I reached an orgasm more powerful than any I had ever experienced. I collapsed on top of her, still inside her, and I was unconscious for two minutes or twenty, and when I awoke I was still in her and still hard and, yes, God help me, I fucked her again.

AND THEN, FINALLY, I realized what I'd done. I'd turned something alive into something dead. I'd taken this life, an innocent life—and whatever experience she'd had in her years hadn't changed her essential innocence.

A man walks into a bar, and an hour later a girl is dead.

Now what?

The urge for self-preservation took over. There was a shovel in the trunk of my car, and in my earlier fantasies, all unfulfilled, I sometimes used it to dig a grave. But now I rejected it as soon as it came to mind. It would take hours, and I didn't have the time. This was a lonely stretch of road, but it wasn't the dark side of the moon, and a couple of cars had swept past me while I lay on her and in her.

She deserved a proper Christian burial, and sooner or later she'd get one, but not now and not from me. I stood up and looked around, and on the other side of the road was a wooded stretch. I picked her up and slung her over my shoulder and crossed the road, and no headlights came swooping out of the darkness while I did so, and then I was in the woods, visible only to owls.

Did an owl hoot? Once, but only in my imagination, on one of the occasions when I replayed the fantasy. But not when I was there, with her weight on my shoulder. A body is said to be heavier after death, though I can't think why this should be so, but dead or alive she was short and slender and didn't weigh very much. I walked twenty or thirty yards into the woods and set her down gently, placing her on her back with her arms at her sides and her legs together.

Sometimes, in fantasy, it's fall and I cover her with leaves. But it was the middle of May and the leaves were still on the trees. I could go back for the blanket, or the clothes I'd torn off of her. But might the blanket somehow be traced back to me? And couldn't the clothes hold a clue? And did I really want to make an extra trip across the road and back?

I left her uncovered. I closed her eyes, as I'd seen doctors do in films, and I moved her hands so that one covered the other. At the solar plexus—perhaps by coincidence, perhaps not.

I went back to where I'd left the car. The blanket, along with her purse and everything she'd been wearing, went in the trunk, and I wasted a moment or two tucking her clothes underneath the blanket, as if that would keep a policeman from noticing them.

Pointless. Unless I was trying to keep myself from noticing them—and still pointless because how could I forget they were there?

I swung the car around, flicked the headlights on long enough to give me a good look at the spot. The spot where she died, the spot where I'd fucked her and killed her.

Killed her and fucked her, more accurately.

HERE'S SOMETHING YOU might not know. I didn't know it myself at the time, and I mean no disrespect by raising the possibility that you're as ignorant as I used to be.

Here it is: Rape and murder, while frequent companions, don't always take place in that order.

Which is to say that I was neither the first nor the last man to kill a girl first and fuck her afterward. If you didn't know this, blame the media; they rarely report it, because it's a little more graphic and specific than convention would prefer.

I have more to tell you about this, but it can wait.

MY HEADLIGHTS DIDN'T show me much. If there was any trace to be seen of what I'd done to her, I certainly couldn't spot it. What I did notice was that, while she may well have been the first person killed in that location, she and I were by no means the first to have had sex there. I counted five condoms, used and tossed aside, including one that must have been under the blanket while I took my pleasure with her.

It probably goes without saying that none of the condoms were mine. I wasn't much worried about getting a dead girl pregnant.

I FOUND MY way out of there by reversing the process I'd used to find the site in the first place. I didn't know where I was, but I drove on that dirt road until I had the opportunity to turn onto a paved road, and from that to a more traveled road. And so on.

I'd spent the seven days in a budget motel with weekly rates, and had checked out that morning because I was ready to quit my job, ready to move on. I stopped at the roadhouse in the hope of finding a woman, and if she hadn't suddenly snapped out of her wine haze, I'd have found some other motel, checked us in, and had sex with her in a proper bed. She might not remember it later, but she'd still have a pulse when she woke up. But I scrapped that plan when she came to and started making a fuss.

Blaming the victim? No, not really. Her behavior changed what followed, but that didn't make it her fault. Driving, eventually reaching a highway, looking left and right for a place to spend what was left of the night, I was wholly aware of whose fault it was.

Mine. Nobody's but mine.

I WAS PROBABLY a hundred miles north of Bakersfield when I found a motel. I paid cash, and was ready to write *John Smith* on the registration card, but the guy behind the counter never offered me one. If I didn't sign in, my twenty dollars could go in his pocket and not in the boss's register.

Fine with me.

First thing I did was take a shower. There were rust stains

in the tub, and the water pressure wasn't all you'd have hoped for, but I ran it hot and wanted to stay under the spray forever. Got out eventually, got as dry as I could with the two little towels they gave you, then supplemented them with a pillowcase. I got the air conditioner to make a sound, although it didn't seem to be cooling the room, and I stretched out on the bed.

Jesus, sweet Jesus, I'd killed a woman. I was a murderer. And a stupid one at that. Anyone who popped my trunk, anyone resourceful enough to look under the blanket, would find the clothes she'd been wearing. And her purse, too, which almost certainly held some ID.

They'd catch me. I'd be tried and convicted. In California, that would mean the gas chamber.

I lay there, waiting for them to kick the door in.

And then my mind wanted something else to think about, so what I turned it to was not the certain consequences of what I'd done but the act itself. Knocking her out. Putting her in the car, hauling her out of the car. Lying on top of her, pinning her to the ground with my weight. My hands around her neck. Choking her, throttling her, strangling her—all those sweet verbs that worked their will upon her until I'd squeezed the life right out of her eyes.

Then stripping her, and slipping into her, and rewarding myself for what I had done.

And I lay naked on that bed, my hair still damp from the shower, and I masturbated not to a fantasy, as I'd done for years, but to something that had actually happened,

something I'd done just a few hours ago. Something I regretted profoundly, something I'd almost certainly pay for with
my life—and something that even in recollection aroused me
beyond my control.

I had an orgasm, my third of the night. Afterward it seems
to me that I felt a wave of unutterable sadness, but I can't be
sure of that. What I do know is that I fell asleep almost immediately, and slept deeply, and without dreams.

WHEN I WOKE up I took another shower. The towels hadn't
dried from the night before, so I used the bed clothing to dry
myself. I thought about what I'd done to her, but I held the
memory at enough of a distance to remain unaroused by it.

Without thinking about it, I put on what I'd worn the
night before. I'd washed her scent off my body, but I could
smell her on my clothes. I wasn't sure how I felt about that.

I thought about the gas chamber. Was there any way to
avoid it?

I drove around, not sure what I was looking for, and in a
strip mall I spotted a collection box for Goodwill Industries.
No one would look too hard or long at a donation. They'd
just launder the clothing and offer it for sale, and some woman somewhere would wear a dead woman's clothes and never
know it.

I pulled up next to the collection box, opened my trunk,
and as I lifted the lid I had the thought that the trunk would

be empty, that the clothing would be gone, that all of this was a false memory.

Yeah, right.

I dropped her clothes in the box, added the blanket. What about her purse? It was black patent leather, scuffed. I'd have to go through it first and remove her ID, but I didn't want to do that now.

Everything I owned was in my duffel bag in the trunk, and I worked the zipper and drew out a change of clothes. With my car screening me from passers-by, I stripped to the skin and put on clean clothes. What I'd taken off—the *Buddy* shirt, the matching work pants, the underwear—went in the Goodwill box with her clothes.

Somebody else could be Buddy.

I got back in the car, drove some more.

I WAS HALFWAY between L.A. and San Francisco, closing in on Santa Barbara, before it dawned on me that I'd stand a better chance if I got out of the state. For a week or two I circled around—Nevada, Colorado, New Mexico, then west again and into Arizona. Most cities had newsstands that carried out-of-town papers, and I bought day-old copies of the two Bakersfield papers, the *Californian* and the *News Observer,* looking for any mention of the discovery of a body, or a missing-persons search for Cindy Raschmann.

I knew her name because I'd finally gone through her

purse. I kept the ninety-two dollars I found in her wallet, and burned everything with her name on it. I dropped the empty purse in one trash bin, the empty wallet in another.

If anyone reported her missing, the Bakersfield papers didn't know about it. But if someone, single and unattached, just stopped showing up—well, somebody might file a missing persons report, and a name and description might go out to area hospitals, but why would the press cover it?

Eight days after I took her throat between my hands, a couple of hikers found the body. A day later, the *News Observer* reported that she'd been identified, and confided that the police were treating the death as a homicide.

You think?

BY THIS TIME I was in a $40-a-week motel outside of Tempe, Arizona. I was getting day work with a moving company and clerking three nights a week at a liquor store in a bad part of town. I figured it was only a matter of time before somebody walked in with a gun, and if he was disappointed enough with what was in the cash register he'd pull the trigger.

Fair enough. Because another thing that was only a matter of time was a couple of uniformed guys knocking on my door. They wouldn't have to get her clothes from the Goodwill or her purse from the trashcan in order to put two and two together. Someone would say, *Yeah, she walked outta here with this young guy, had some size on him.* And someone else could say, *Sure, I saw the two of them, he had one of those shirts like you'll see at a Sunoco station. Kind with his name on the pocket? Buddy, that's what it said.* And after they checked enough Sunoco stations, somebody would remember a guy with *Buddy* on his shirt pocket. *Guy worked regular, and then one day he didn't show up. Didn't bring the shirt back, either.*

One thing leading to another, the way they do.

So I waited for the knock to come, waited for the world to fall apart, waited to start a long walk with a gas chamber at the end of it. When I wasn't working one job or the other, I sat in my motel room and thought about the gas chamber. All I really knew about it was from watching Susan Hayward play Barbara Graham in *I Want to Live.*

There's an interesting story about Barbara Graham. Can't swear it's true, but I'd like to believe it.

We'll get to it.

I KEPT BUYING the Bakersfield papers, as if they'd know about my arrest before I did. But I didn't see anything about Cindy Raschmann aside from the occasional back-page item reporting that Bakersfield police, assisted by state troopers, were continuing to pursue unspecified leads in the matter. Just a matter of time, they said, and I'd already worked that part out for myself.

But most of the paper was devoted to the upcoming California primary. The country would be electing a president in

November, and California looked to be a swing state for the
Democratic candidates. And on the fifth of June voters went
to the polls, and within hours of his being declared the victor,
Robert F. Kennedy was shot dead by a little guy who liked his
name so much he used it twice. Good he did the deed in L.A.,
and not, say, Walla Walla.

1968, THIS WAS. Years and years ago, and I'm telling you the
story, so you should be able to figure out that the knock on
the door never came, that I got away with it.

Took me a while to believe it. It looked as though I actually had a second shot at life, but how could I trust it? How did
I know it wasn't some celestial joke, some cosmic prankster
building me up only to knock me down?

I mean, I'd killed a girl. You don't get a pass on something
like that.

Do you?

DAYS PASSED, AND I could see that was what had happened.
The assassination took everybody's mind off the murder of
a woman with no relatives or close friends to pester the Bakersfield cops for updates on the investigation. The case went
cold.

It was hard for me to know what to make of it. I'd come close to resigning myself to the punishment I knew I deserved, and now it looked as though there wasn't going to be any punishment, and that idea took some getting used to.

I had a life back. What was I going to do with it?

FOR THE TIME being, I could just keep on keeping on. Working moving jobs when they called me, working nights at the liquor store. It must have been early July when a customer walked in an hour before closing and spent a long time checking out different brands of whiskey.

I knew there was something wrong with him.

I waited on another customer, a guy with a limp who came in every evening around that time to pick up a pint of Schenley's. He could have bought it by the quart and reduced the wear and tear on his bad hip by fifty percent, but maybe this gave him an excuse to get out of the house.

He limped out, and as soon as the door closed behind him, Mr. Wrong approached the counter with a fifth of Chivas in one hand and a gun in the other.

Well, didn't that just fucking figure? Get off one hook and life comes at you with another.

I was way too angry to be afraid. "Oh, go ahead and shoot me," I told him, even as I reached to grab a bottle of wine off the shelf. "Go ahead, you son of a bitch! You think I give a rat's ass?"

I marched straight toward him, brandishing the wine bottle and waiting for the gunshot. But what he did was drop the gun, hold on to the bottle of Chivas. And run out the door.

I DIDN'T KNOW what to do with the gun. Call the cops? No, I don't think so. I picked the thing up without getting my prints on it or disturbing his, and I put it on the shelf beneath the counter, alongside the billy club the owner kept there. I might have picked that up, instead of the wine bottle, but if I'd been thinking that clearly to begin with I'd have hit NO SALE and let him clean out the register.

I locked up when I was supposed to, and when I left I had the gun with me, in one of the paper bags meant to hold a pint bottle of wine or whiskey. I didn't know what I wanted it for, but thought it might be more of a mistake to leave it behind than to take it with me. I drove straight back to my motel, took a shower, got into bed, and waited for the fear to flood in after the fact. But that didn't happen. Once again I had my life back, and it was up to me to figure out what to do with it.

I thought about Cindy Raschmann, who hadn't gotten her life back, and never would. I'd thought of her often, with variable results. Sometimes I was overcome with guilt and shame, and the hopeless desire to undo what I had done. But on other occasions all I could think of was the sheer ecstasy of it all.

This time, perhaps as a reaction to looking down the barrel of a gun, the eroticism prevailed. I relived the incident, improving it by calling her by her name, which of course I hadn't known at the time. In fantasy I fastened duct tape over her mouth, and toyed with her by pinching her nostrils shut, then letting her gasp for breath. Over and over again, until her struggles so aroused me that I got my hands on her throat, even as I'd done in actuality.

And so on.

Delicious, all of it. The real recollection, the fantasized improvements. No matter how much I genuinely regretted it, it was all a part of who I was.

And would forever be.

SO SHOULD I then look for another roadhouse and pick up another young woman who'd had too much to drink? Maybe I'd keep this one alive for a while. Let her struggle, let her know what was coming. Maybe fuck her first and then kill her.

Maybe not. Maybe stick with what works.

I imagined myself as a serial killer, although the term itself would not come into vogue for several more years. (The behavior had existed for centuries, and perhaps forever. Who's to say what Cain got up to after he went off on his own?) But the language took its time catching up.

I mean, wasn't that the logical way for me to behave? I'd

done the foul deed, I'd enjoyed it and been transported by it beyond all expectations, and I'd gone on to spend many of my waking hours (and God knows how much of my dream time) savoring the experience, relishing the memory, enhancing it in fantasy. Over and over Cindy Raschmann died, over and over I spilled my seed in her insensate body, over and over and over.

Wouldn't she, sooner or later, lose her charm?

A MAN WALKS into a bar.

A downtown bar, a place to relax after a day at the office. When the office crowd thinned out, the clientele changed. Serious drinkers, men and women looking for a cure for loneliness. The occasional semipro hooker.

I'd been in there a few times, scouting the place. Always sat alone at the bar, always had a scotch and soda. Never spoke to anyone, except to order my drink. Never said or did anything memorable.

Thought about it, though. Took some of the female patrons home, if only in my mind. One was a frequent star in my fantasies, a housewife who'd come in for a quick one before she drove one kid to a soccer game or picked up another from a play date. A MILF, you'd call her nowadays, though no one had yet come up with the term. There were plenty of MILFs, but nobody knew what to call them.

Like serial killers. Abundant, but not yet labeled.

Taller than Cindy Raschmann, and a few years older, and with a fuller figure. Unconvincing red hair, so the carpet probably didn't match the drapes.

Never mind. She was hot, and she had a restlessness about her that was appealing.

She'd do.

WOULD IT HAVE been soccer that her kid played? I don't think the game had yet caught on, certainly not in Arizona, nor do I think she'd have called her other kid's afternoon engagement a play date. The boy was probably playing baseball. His sister was doing homework at a friend's house.

Like it matters.

Soccer games and play dates. MILFs—or should that be MILVES?

Serial killers.

A MAN WALKS into a bar, and the MILF of his dreams is there, and sitting by herself. Sitting at one of the little tables, the glass in front of her almost empty.

I got a J&B and soda at the bar. "And let me have another of what Red's having."

He smiled. "Red's name is Carolyn," he said, reaching and

pouring and stirring. "And what she's having is an Orange Blossom."

I took both glasses to her table, dropped into the empty chair, raised my own glass in a toast. "Well now," she said, and picked up the stemmed glass that held her Orange Blossom. "What are we drinking to?"

"To the future," I said. "May it have Carolyn in it."

"And may it be better than the past," she said, and took a sip. "You know my name."

"And all it cost me was the price of a drink."

"But I don't know yours."

"You're better off that way," I said. "I tend to forget it myself. People generally call me Buddy."

"Then that's what I'll call you," she said.

And we talked, and she found excuses to touch me—the back of my hand, my arm. I put a hand on her knee and she didn't pull away. I looked a question into her eyes and she answered with a slow smile.

To the future, I'd said, and I could see it all right there in front of me.

"Back in a minute," I said, and headed for the men's room. And walked past it, and out the back door. I'd already checked out of my motel, and everything I owned was in the trunk of my car.

Along with a new blanket, a roll of duct tape, and an icepick.

Drove to the closest on-ramp, got on the Interstate. Kept it just under the speed limit, just as I'd have done if I'd left Carolyn with a crushed windpipe and a belly full of semen.

Instead I'd left her with half an Orange Blossom, most of a J&B and soda, and all the time in the world to wonder what she'd said that turned me off.

Hard one for either of us to answer.

Crossed a state line, found a motel. Checked in, had another shower. Got in bed.

Thought about my MILF. This time we left the bar together, and drove to her house, which I chose to situate in a suburban cul-de-sac. Immobilized her with the duct tape, but left her mouth untaped because I wanted to be able to hear her scream.

I made sure the houses were far apart. No one would hear her screams.

And so on.

I WAS GOING to tell you about Barbara Graham.

Not the part you can read on Wikipedia. Mother a prostitute, Barbara in the game herself early on. The company of career criminals, and three or four or five of them heard of a woman who was supposed to keep a lot of money around the house. And they broke in, and the woman wouldn't give up the money, and Barbara pistol-whipped her and suffocated her with a pillow.

Or she didn't. She said she didn't but what would you expect her to say?

The crime went down in March of 1953. On June 3, 1955,

after an appeal and a very brief stay of execution, they led her to the gas chamber. Somebody told her it would make it easier for her if she took a deep breath as soon as the cyanide pellets were dropped. Her response: "How the hell would you know, you silly rascal?"

You really think she said *silly rascal?* The woman's last words, and some city editor felt the need to clean them up. "How the hell would you know, you fucking moron?"

Sounds more like it.

But none of that is the point. It's all background, and most of it probably true, for a story that's far less verifiable. There was this man, his name lost to history, who boasted that he was the last man ever to fuck her.

She had been locked up in the women's prison in Chino, but they transferred her to San Quentin, where she spent a single night on Death Row before they gassed her. And there was this trusty, a man doing straight life in San Quentin for who knows what, and he was tasked with cleaning the lethal chamber after the execution had been carried out. Which I suppose involved hosing down this and wiping up that, after he'd removed the dead body.

Well, you see where this is going. Here she was, not merely hot-looking but something of a celebrity, and she'd been dead for what, ten minutes? Fifteen minutes?

Still warm and still fresh, so he took a few minutes to fuck her.

No way she could fight him off, not once she'd taken that deep breath. No way anyone else would be around to watch, because it was an unpleasant task they'd been eager to palm off on a prisoner. A couple of minutes of in and out, and after he'd made a deposit in her cashbox, he'd move the body where they'd told him. And then he'd hose down this and wipe up that.

And afterward he could tell all his friends about it. *"You know what I did, man? Think you can't have any pussy in prison? Well, think again."*

Maybe he did it, just like he said. Maybe he never did it, but got off on telling the story. Or maybe he never existed in the first place, maybe a couple of prison guards carried her out on a stretcher, and someone else made up a story a month or a year later. Once somebody told it, you can see how it would tend to get repeated.

So buy it or not, as you prefer, and I don't see how anyone could prove it one way or the other. Certainly not at this late date.

Still, I like to think it's true.

OF COURSE I remembered the case. I was in my early teens when they gassed her, and it was years later before I heard the story about the upstanding citizen who'd been her last lover. But I knew what they printed in the papers, and a couple of years later I got to see Susan Hayward play her in the film.

A fine-looking woman, Susan Hayward. Judging from the photos, you could say as much for Barbara Graham.

I DON'T KNOW what it was that saved my MILF. Possibly our conversation, which forced me to reclassify her from object to person. Or perhaps it was in the cards. Perhaps, like college basketball stars opting for the NBA draft, I was one and done.

I can certainly see how it could have gone the other way. I'd gotten away with murder, and not because I was a criminal genius, always a step ahead of the police. I'd blundered into a crime, blundered through it, and blundered out of it, with nothing beyond dumb luck guiding my footsteps.

Another man—or my own self, on another day—might have decided if I'd gotten away with it once I could get away with it twice, and three times, and four.

And so on.

What I decided was the reverse. *Don't push your luck,* I told myself. *Take what happened and tuck it away, out of sight but not out of mind. Enjoy it in memory, for as long as you can. Transform it into fantasy if you will. But don't do it again.*

How many men can take that advice? How many of us can cross a forbidden line once and never step over it again?

That might as well be a rhetorical question, because how could anyone possibly answer that? No one's keeping stats on those of us who are one and done.

And if we relive those moments, if we take other victims in the privacy of our own minds, well, that won't put us on any lists, either. So I don't know how many men commit such an act once and never repeat it, don't know if our numbers are many or few.

But I know this much. I managed it.

I SPENT A few days driving, heading generally north and east, staying in budget motels, entertaining myself with poetry.

I'm thinking of Wordsworth's definition, of which I was entirely ignorant at the time: "*Poetry is the spontaneous overflow of powerful feelings: it takes its origin from emotion recollected in tranquility.*" In the tranquility of my motel room, with the TV off and the door locked and the shades down, I would recall what had happened with Cindy, and what might have happened with Carolyn.

Powerful feelings, to be sure. Not to mention spontaneous overflow.

Each morning I arose and got behind the wheel, each evening found myself another motel. One night outside of Peoria I checked in and walked across the road to a Denny's. *Breakfast any time!* the menu proclaimed, and I sat at the counter and tucked into their Hungry Man's Breakfast, only to discover I didn't have appetite enough to finish it.

But I lingered over a second cup of coffee, not out of a desire for it but because I liked the looks of the waitress. A brunette, and on the plump side, but with something saucy about her.

Aside from ordering my meal, I never said a word to her. Not even to order the coffee, or later to ask for the check. I pointed to the cup and she filled it. I scribbled in the air and she brought the check.

Later that night, she was the unwitting star of my little movie.

Worked fine.

TO MAKE THIS life change work, it had to be more than a matter of living in memory and fantasy while keeping reality at bay. That was clear to me. I had to become a different person—or, more accurately, I had to create a different life for myself.

I'm not much inclined to get into it, but you would almost have to wonder what made me the way I am. One's used to the normal components—raging alcoholic father, domineering mother, sexually abusive parent or uncle or priest or scoutmaster or trusted family friend. "Why is this man a monster? Because his childhood was monstrous."

Not mine.

Ours was an oversized family—six sons, four daughters—but neither abusive nor dysfunctional. My father owned and oversaw an insurance agency, the town's largest, and while I was in high school began offering mutual funds as well. My mother, with ten children under her care, never considered a career outside the home, though the needlework she entered in contests frequently won prizes.

I was a desultory student, often lost in thought and consequently unprepared when called on. But I did well enough on tests to balance it all out, and my grades were average.

I joined the Boy Scouts, hoping for camping trips, but our troop was more interested in saluting and marching, as if it might find its true calling as a chapter of the Hitler Youth. A few months was enough, and I dropped out. But not because our scoutmaster (who, now that I think about it, bore a distinct resemblance to Adolf Eichmann) ever laid a finger on me.

Nor did the teachers at the Sunday school we all attended. I didn't last long there, either. My brother Henry told my mother that he hated it, and did he have to go? She said he didn't, and I said I hated it too, although I merely thought it was tedious. So Henry and I never went back, which is not to say that we played together while our brothers and sisters learned more than anybody needs to know about Mary Magdalene and Lazarus. Henry, Hank to his friends, was four years older than I, and found me at least as dull as Sunday school.

If there was one thing that stood out about our family, it's how little apparent interest we had in each other. I guess my father was proud to have so many children, even as he was proud he was able to support us all. But that was about as far as his interest went. And I guess my mother was, well, maternal—albeit in a way that you couldn't call motherly. She did the cooking and, with the assistance of a twice-a-week housekeeper, kept house. Made sure we had our shots, made sure there were clean clothes in our dresser drawers. Put dinner on the table and saw to it that we ate it. All in a manner I've since realized was dispassionate: We were her children, and she was supposed to take care of us, and she was a woman who did what she was supposed to do. And so she did.

My older sisters helped, Judy and Rhea, born less than a year apart. Irish twins, I'd heard them called, though I had no idea why. Arnie showed up a year later. I was fifth in the birth order, the third boy, four years younger than Hank, who was himself two and a half years younger than Arnie. Then four more years passed before the next birth, a sister named Charlotte.

And to which of them was I closest?

None of them, really.

I had to think to write that paragraph with their names, Arnie and Hank and Charlotte. I barely remember them, my clutch of siblings. There were four more after Charlotte, and I think they were an even mix of boys and girls, but I can't recall their order of birth, or even their names. Ten all told, so many of us you'd have thought we would have to have been Catholic, but we belonged in fact to some bland Protestant denomination.

Maybe my parents were ignorant or slipshod when it came to birth control.

Maybe they actually wanted us. Though I can't imagine why.

TWICE I ALMOST left the gun behind.

A day or two after I acquired it, when I took it from its pint-of-whiskey paper bag for perhaps the tenth time, still holding it so as to avoid disturbing the previous owner's fingerprints or imposing my own, it occurred to me that it might be dangerous for me to be in possession of it. I sniffed it, wondering if it had been fired since its last cleaning, but all I smelled was metal; if either gun oil or gun powder residue were present, my nose couldn't spot them.

I put it back in its paper bag, stowed it for the time being on the motel room's closet shelf. It could stay there, I decided, until someone found it, and it might be someone other than the maid, because she'd need to be taller than average to reach it.

I went to bed, and in the morning I changed my mind and took the weapon with me when I left.

A few days later, I packed up and was out the door of another motel when I remembered I'd neglected to retrieve the thing from the dresser drawer where I'd stowed it. I remember standing there, half in and half out of the door, unsure what to do. I went back for it, and this time I stashed it in the glove compartment.

BY THE TIME I let Greyhound drive me across the Ohio state line I was a different person.

Literally. At least to the extent that I had an Indiana

driver's license in a new name. I was now John James Thompson, a far more common name than the one I'd been born with. That was my choice. I didn't want to stand out.

It used to be remarkably easy to change one's identity. When the American West was the frontier, all you had to do was ride into town and give your name. No one would ask to see your ID, because the whole concept barely existed. You didn't need a license to ride a horse. There were no Social Security cards, even as there was no Social Security. You got to be whoever you claimed to be, and unless trouble followed you from your old life, your new name could be yours for as long as you wanted.

It was still pretty easy in 1968. You learned the name of some unfortunate child who'd died young, ideally in infancy, claimed his name for your own, and requested a copy of your birth certificate. I might have been Clarence Glendower or Peter Kowalski, but rejected the first as too distinctive and the second as too ethnic. Little Johnny Thompson had survived infancy, but his gravestone reported that he'd died a month shy of his fifth birthday. And he'd been born just over two years after me, on the fourteenth of June.

June fourteenth is Flag Day, and while the Thompson lad hadn't lived long enough to wave any flags, or have any raised in his honor, the holiday made it easy to reel off my new date of birth when asked.

Over time, of course, it was the other way around. After not too many years I was for a fact John James Thompson, and my birthday helped me to remember when Flag Day was.

The only downside, really, was that usurping JJT's date of birth made me two years younger than I was in actuality. And what was the matter with that? Well, for a long time it was fine. But the time came when I had to wait an extra two years before I could collect Social Security.

I PICKED UP my birth certificate and a Social Security card in Indianapolis, then drove to Fort Wayne, where I took a test and got an Indiana driver's license for my new name. My car was registered to my old name, and I thought about selling it to myself, but decided that would leave a trail. I sold it instead to a used car dealer, took a bus from Forth Wayne to Lima, Ohio, and bought a used Plymouth Valiant off a dealer's lot. The following afternoon I took another test and traded in my Indiana license for an Ohio one.

I never actually picked Lima as my new home, and I might have moved on and gone further east, possibly all the way to the coast. But things started falling into place.

I was staying at first in a motel, and got into a conversation with the guy on the desk, who told me about the Rodeway Inn a quarter of a mile away. Their night man had quit abruptly and they were looking to replace him.

And I was looking to earn back some of the money I'd been spending on meals and motels, and the couple of hundred I was out of pocket swapping my car for the Valiant. I assured the manager at the Rodeway that I didn't drink, didn't mind working nights, and had no use for Democrats or Coloreds, and that got me a room and a salary. Both were on the small side, but I could live with that.

And one thing led to another.

I thought of my father, who'd joined Kiwanis and Rotary and the Lions Club, and not out of a sense of civic duty. "The contacts are important," I'd heard him say, and something clicked when I learned that Rotary met once a week in a conference room right there at the Rodeway. I found a men's shop and bought a blue blazer and a shirt and tie, and took a deep breath and walked into the next meeting, figuring the worst that could happen was they'd ask me to leave.

They didn't. I went every week, and one day maybe three or four weeks in a portly fellow asked me what line of work I was in. I said I was new in town, and for the time being I was on the desk nights in that very motel. "It's honest work," I said, "but, well   "

"But not much chance of advancement," he said. "You know who's looking for someone?" He pointed at a rail-thin man on the far side of the room. "Porter Dawes," he said. "Man could hide behind a straw, but he'll treat you right. You know him? C'mon, John. Be my pleasure to introduce you."

Dawes was in the hardware and housewares business, and within a few minutes so was I. After two years he made me the manager, and two years after that cancer took him down. When he knew he wasn't going to get better, he sat me down with his lawyer, and we drew up an agreement for me to buy the business from his widow, paying a small amount down and the rest out of earnings. She'd also participate directly in profits, but as owner I'd get the lion's share.

"I'm glad to have that settled," he said after we'd signed it. "Now I can die in peace." And a month later he did just that.

BY THEN I was a member of Kiwanis and the Lions as well, and if I didn't get to every meeting I was active enough to be on a first-name basis with a sizable portion of Lima's business and professional class. The store had always been profitable, but I made a couple of changes after I took over, and signed on a fellow Rotarian to develop an ad campaign. Profits went up.

I guess people noticed, and a white-haired man named Ewell Kennerly asked me if I'd thought about Penderville. All I knew about it was that it was a ways south of town on I-75.

"I'll tell you," he said, "the place is a real boomtown. Ethel and I moved there when the kids finished college, and we love it. If you're fixing to expand, you ought to consider it."

It hadn't occurred to me to expand. I had the one store, I made a fair living from it.

"A nasty divorce went and put a good auto parts store out of business, and as a result there's a beautiful retail site looking for a tenant. And if you don't want to sink a lot of dough into it, well, I've done real well over the years as a silent partner. It's a role I enjoy." He patted me on the shoulder. "Something to think about," he said. "Why stay small when it's so easy to

grow? And if Louella has a boy, won't be too many years before he can be your manager. Or was that something I wasn't
supposed to know?"

LOUELLA.

Outside of the privacy of my own mind, there'd been no
women in my life.

By the time I got to Lima, I had closed that door and
locked it. Now and then, at work or away from it, I might
find myself in casual conversation with an attractive woman.
Or I'd see someone—a diner at another table in a restaurant,
a customer at the store—and I'd be drawn to her.

I kept the door locked. I had a sufficient understanding
of my inner self to know I didn't dare open it. I had already
been through as much as I ever wanted to go through. I'd had
the great misfortune of acting on my impulses and the result
had been the death of an innocent woman; then I'd had the
astonishingly good fortune to get away with it.

I'd been given a second chance. I wouldn't get a third.

And, you know, temptation got easier to resist with the
passage of time. The incident in Bakersfield kept slipping further into the past. It became less and less a part of my essential
self.

Besides, let us not forget, I was growing older, one day at a
time. The urges that drive a man, for better or for worse, tend
to subside with time.

Oh, I could still be stirred by the sight of an attractive woman. And I still took my memories and fantasies to bed, though with a good deal less urgency. Memories tended to dim with time, and increasingly I gave myself over less to what I remembered and more to what I could only imagine.

A woman glimpsed from a car window, playing an unwitting role a night or two later in an event of pure imagination. The young mother of a childhood friend, conjured up out of the past, and when I thought of her now I found myself endowing her with some of the attributes of Carolyn—she who drank Orange Blossoms, she who could never have known how close she came to pain and death.

There had been a time, it seemed to me, when I thought of little else. Hard to apportion credit for the change—or blame, as you prefer. Age would certainly account for some of it, but so it seemed would habit. I'd made it a habit to hold that part of myself in check, and now I no longer needed a tight grip on the reins.

Then Myron Hendricksen changed things when he put his hand on my thigh.

HE WAS A few years younger than I, a few pounds heavier, an inch or two shorter. He was a pharmacist who owned his own drugstore. He belonged to Rotary, and to one or two other clubs as well. He lived—

But it doesn't matter where he lived. It doesn't really matter who he was. What does matter is that I was in the steam room at the gym, sharing the space with two other fellows, when Myron Hendricksen came in and took a seat next to me on the wooden bench.

All was wholly unremarkable until the other men left. Then Myron broke the silence by starting a conversation. I don't remember what it was about, I didn't pay much attention to it, but I did note that he seemed a little nervous, a bit uneasy.

And then he laid a hand on my thigh. I had a white towel wrapped around my waist, as did he, and before I could react to the presence of his hand, or begin to grasp what was going on, it moved upward a few inches.

"What the hell!"

He withdrew his hand. I looked at him and watched his face fall. "Oh God," he said. "I thought, oh dear God, I don't know what I thought."

Whatever it was, he'd have to wait to voice it, as right around then the door opened and two other men entered, talking about the relative merits of the Cleveland Browns and the Cincinnati Bengals.

I stood up and got out of there. Stood under the shower for a minute or so, then went to my locker. I was in no hurry, and by the time I was dressed he had emerged from the steam room. I took a step in his direction and saw him recoil in fear.

I said, "We have to talk."

He nodded.

"In the coffee shop on the corner."

I went there myself, took a booth off to the side. A waitress brought me my coffee and I let it sit. It was still untouched when Myron came in, looked around, and forced himself to come over. He stood at the side of the booth and said, "Please don't hit me."

"Sit down," I said. "Why would I hit you?"

"Because I groped you. I honestly thought—"

"That I would welcome it?"

"I thought you were—"

"Gay? I'm not."

"That became very clear," he said. "God, the look on your face. Like you couldn't believe it."

"Well," I said, "I couldn't."

There was a silence that lasted until the waitress came over. He ordered something. When she left he told me more than I needed to know about him. How he was respectable, how he was married, how he loved his wife and adored his children, and how he was attracted to men and sometimes felt compelled to act on this attraction.

"I'm very careful," he said.

"So you must have thought I'd be receptive."

"Well—"

He considered his response. "I suppose the wish was father to the thought," he said. "You're a very attractive man."

"If you were to make a pass at every man you found attractive—"

"I'd be dead or in jail." He drew a breath. "John, there was nothing about you to announce that you were gay, nothing in your manner or your dress. I never saw you look at other men with desire."

"I've never been attracted to men."

"But there were other signs to read. I thought, you know, that you were in the same boat I'm in. Deeply closeted, keeping a dark secret and desperate that no one find it out."

Which was not untrue, I thought. But it was not the secret he wanted it to be.

The waitress brought him his sandwich. Did I want a refill on the coffee? I assured her I was fine.

He said, "In all the time I've known you, all the time I've been aware of you, I've never seen any indication that you're interested in women."

Really?

"You're not married, you don't have a girlfriend, and I've never seen you in a woman's company. If a man's not interested in women—"

"Then he must be interested in men?"

"Well, what else is there?"

"Sheep," I suggested, and it took him a moment to realize I'd just made a joke. Once he did, he gave it a heartier laugh than it deserved, more out of relief than amusement. If I could make a joke, then perhaps all of this was less likely to end with him exposed to his friends, or punched in the mouth.

"For the record," I said, "I'm exclusively heterosexual. And you're quite correct, I haven't been involved with anyone since I turned up in Lima."

He waited, while I considered how to go on.

"There was a woman," I said. "We were very much in love. It ended badly."

"She broke it off with you?"

"In the worst way possible, Myron. She died."

Well, that part was true.

HE COULDN'T HAVE been more sympathetic, or more apologetic for having read grief as forbidden desire. And, after I'd assured him that his secret was safe with me, he begged me not to hate him.

"Hate you? Why on earth would I hate you?"

"Because—"

"Because you found me attractive? That's a compliment, not an insult. If anything, I've got reason to be grateful to you."

"Oh?"

"You've helped me realize something," I said. "My mourning, my devotion to a lost love, all of that was genuine enough. But over time it's ossified into habit. It's time I got back in the game."

AND SO I did. Cautiously, tentatively. I'd ask one woman out to dinner, take another to the movies. I took pains to appear at ease on such occasions, and to a certain extent I was, but a part of my mind was always busy taking my emotional temperature. Did I like this woman? Did I find her attractive?

Was conversation with her difficult or easy? Interesting or tedious? Did I want to see her again?

More to the point, did I want to fuck her? Did I want to kill her first and *then* fuck her?

Sometimes I asked myself what the hell I thought I was doing. My life in Lima was pleasant enough. I was making decent money, and my prospects were good. I had a growing circle of acquaintances with whom I could contrive to spend as much or as little time as I wanted.

I wouldn't say that I had any friends. But then I had never had a friend, and how could I be expected to make one now?

I'd seen this bit of doggerel in a souvenir shop, burned into a wooden plaque:

A friend is not a fellow who is taken in by sham
A friend is one who knows our faults and doesn't give a damn

So there you have it. My acquaintances could only be fellows taken in by sham, as I did not dare to let anyone know who I really was. Because they'd certainly give a damn. How could they not?

Did any of them assume I was homosexual?

Myron had made that assumption, and risked a great deal to act on it. "I suppose the wish was father to the thought," he'd said, and it very likely was. But, its paternity notwithstanding, the thought itself had sprung too from an observation of the way I lived my life.

Perhaps other men, and women as well, were wondering if I might be gay. As far as I could tell, there were no signs pointing actively in that direction. I didn't utter sentences with every fourth word italicized, I didn't dress flamboyantly, I'd never argued the superiority of ballet to baseball. You could search my apartment from top to bottom and never turn up so much as a single Judy Garland record.

Still, aside from business, I was never seen in the company of women. I was a bachelor, and my lifestyle was less that of the eligible bachelor (which is code for a single man who pursues women) than that of the confirmed bachelor (which is code for one who eschews their company entirely).

Did it matter what they thought?

I couldn't think why it should, and yet it seemed beyond dispute that it did.

I wondered why.

WAS I GAY? Some version of gay?

If so, I'd gone an awful lot of years without even entertaining the thought. I tried without much success to entertain it now. I couldn't begin to conjure up a fantasy involving Myron, or indeed any of the local businessmen and professionals of my acquaintance. So I made up a young man out of the whole cloth—or perhaps *out of the whole flesh* is a more suitable phrase. Tall, well built, blond hair, blue eyes, skin lightly tanned by the sun. Slim waist, broad shoulders.

A large penis, a small penis? Circumcised? I couldn't really bring that subject into focus, so I let it remain vague.

I tried to imagine the two of us in a motel room, performing various acts upon one another. The fantasies were at best unconvincing, at worst faintly distasteful. I couldn't even maintain them in my mind; my thoughts kept drifting away to wholly asexual topics.

So much for that, I thought.

Then one night, after a not unpleasant evening with a divorced woman—dinner at an ostensibly Italian restaurant, then a movie, finally a near-kiss on her doorstep—it struck me that I wasn't giving my fantasy a fair chance.

I took myself home, had a shower, poured a drink. Went to bed.

And now I willed my imaginary partner to be younger and smaller and less muscular. Just a boy, really, somewhere in his mid to late teens, standing by the side of the road with his thumb out. A hitchhiker.

Hitchhiker fantasies were always good. A girl on her way home from college. Cut-off jeans, a blouse with a couple of buttons unbuttoned. A quick move, a choke hold to put her to sleep. A detour, ending in a spot not unlike the lovers' lane where Cindy Raschmann sacrificed her life for the greater good.

And so on.

So this was my fantasy, an experiment, and I gave it a fair chance. I let it play out in detail, let the boy come to the awful realization that this man who'd given him a ride intended to give him a ride of another sort.

A hard fist in the solar plexus, a quick choke hold, and a

moment where I took his chin in one hand and gripped his hair with the other, ready to snap his neck.

But no, let it wait. Drive him to that predetermined location, drag him out of the car, get him out of his clothes. Wait for him to wake up, penetrate him, and then choke the life out of him. Gaze into his eyes. Watch the light die in them.

No, I couldn't sustain it, not even in fantasy. If I felt anything, beyond a faint sense of revulsion, it was a great disconnect of self from the scenario I was compelling myself to envision.

It was like watching television and sitting through a deodorant commercial, waiting for it to be over.

A JOKE, AND I don't know where or when I heard it. I recall it as having been told in an English accent, although I don't know that it would have to be.

"I say, did you hear about Carruthers?"

"Carruthers? No, I can't say I have."

"It seems he's been caught buggering a giraffe."

"A giraffe!"

"A giraffe."

"Buggering the beast, you say?"

"So it would appear."

"How could he—"

"I'm told a ladder was involved."

"Extraordinary. Um, I say—"

"Yes?"

"Male or female giraffe, do you happen to know?"

"Oh, female, of course. Nothing queer about Carruthers."

LOUELLA, THEN.

After a few months as an eligible bachelor, it began to dawn on me what I was doing. I was looking for someone to marry.

It seems obvious now. I didn't need a woman's company to hide my homosexuality from the world, and for two reasons: I wasn't homosexual, and it didn't really matter if people were to wonder, and draw their own conclusions. I could largely spike that, if I wanted, by letting a few other people in on the confidence I'd shared with Myron Hendricksen, that I was mourning a lost love and staying true to her memory. That sort of word gets around, and while it might lead some of Lima's widows and grass widows to set their caps for me, it would make it easy for me to smile a sad smile and disengage.

He's not ready yet, they'd say. *He must have really loved her*, they'd say. *And oh, what a lucky woman she must have been!*

Ah yes. The luck of Cindy Raschmann...

Never mind. Cindy Raschmann was a long time ago. Cindy Raschmann was long since buried or cremated, and whatever people had known her would by now have trouble remembering what she looked like, or much of anything about her.

More to the point, I was no longer the man who had killed her. He and I may have had the same fingerprints, the same DNA, but how could you argue that we were the same person?

I'd been a drifter, an accident looking for a place to happen. A man wearing somebody else's work shirt with somebody else's nickname on the pocket. Was there ever a guy named Buddy, a guy who walked into a bar and walked out looking for trouble?

If there was, he was long gone.

Otherwise there would be more bodies. That's what guys like Buddy Shirt-Pockets did, they kept doing what they got off on, sometimes recklessly, sometimes carefully, but they didn't stop. How could they stop? Why ever would they want to?

I would read about them, you know. I'm not sure who buys books about serial killers. Women looking to be either frightened or somehow reassured? Men who want to explore from the safe distance of the library what they secretly yearn to do themselves?

And so I read about them, Ted Bundy and Ed Kemper and no end of men whose names you wouldn't know, unless your bookshelf had the same volumes on it as mine. Ted and Ed—and how curious that we know them by their nicknames—were particular favorites, although that may not be the right word for it. I mean, of course, that I devoured books about them, read everything I could find.

Sometimes, I'll admit, prurient interest played a role. Sometimes I found their behavior exciting, and took their exploits to bed with me, in a manner of speaking. But it was more a matter of wanting to know what they were about. Not the childhood trauma that got them started, but how they'd lived after they'd evolved into monsters.

Bundy and Kemper (or Ted and Ed, as you prefer) were two who reversed the usual order of sex and murder. The act of murder was a means to an end, a method of obtaining a sexual partner. (Again, that may not be the right word.) The killing was aphrodisiacal, even thrilling, but the payoff came post-mortem.

Someone—and it may have been Ted or it may have been Ed or it may have been someone else—confided that the absolute best sex consisted of anal intercourse with a woman whom one had strangled within the past half hour. Vaginal intercourse, he contended, came a close second.

Then again, sex with the dead can be dictated by circumstance. A spur-of-the-moment decision, if you will. An impulse purchase.

A pair of cousins, known collectively as the Hillside Strangler, were sadists, torturing their victims while having sex with them. And on at least one occasion (unless this was the writer's invention) ten minutes or so after they'd capped off a couple of hours of rape and torture by wringing the woman's neck, one of them remarked, "Jesus, she's still hot!"

And fucked her again.

LOUELLA.

I keep starting to tell you about her, and seem incapable of following through. Instead I continue wandering off on tangents. Not that these side roads are without interest, to be sure, but—

Enough.

I was long done with the life of the homicidal rover. Increasingly, I found it hard to imagine myself in that role. And I wanted nothing so much as to establish myself as the person I would hope others would believe me to be.

Is that too abstract?

Let's try again. I wanted my fellows—my neighbors, my fellow Rotarians, my business associates, my clientele—to see me as a quiet but sociable middle-class gentleman, a tad conservative in politics and demeanor and dress, indeed a pillar of the established order.

And, more to the point, I didn't want it to be an act. I wanted genuinely to be that person.

So I wanted a wife. Children. A house—it didn't have to be very grand, but ought to be an attractive and welcoming house, nicely landscaped, with flower beds and a well-kept lawn.

The dates I had—dinner and a movie, more often than not—started out as façade and changed without my conscious intent into auditions. Before I even knew it, I was looking for a woman to join me in that cozy little house, someone to plant bulbs in the garden while I raked the lawn. Once I realized as much, I understood why I rarely saw any of the women a second time, and none of them more than twice.

They were pleasant company, presentable and even attractive. Most had been married at some point, though a few had not, but I had the feeling throughout that none of them would be averse to a trip to the altar, should the right man be so inclined.

Or a trip to bed, for that matter. More than one evening concluded with an invitation to come in for a cup of coffee. More than one woman managed to find an excuse to touch my arm or the back of my hand, at once establishing intimacy and inviting further intimacy.

I left the invitations unaccepted, and hoped I managed to seem oblivious to what was on offer. "Oh, I had too much coffee earlier," I might say. Or otherwise invent a reason why I had to go home.

And did I end such evenings by casting my dinner partners in fantasies? Curiously, I did not. Most evenings I read myself to sleep, and with something far less inflammatory than my books on Ed and Ted and their fellows. An English mystery, perhaps, or one of those enthusiastic volumes that would tell you how to grow your business by visualizing success, or developing a positive attitude, or making a list each evening of five steps you'd taken that day to bring you closer to your goals.

Whatever they might be.

LOUELLA SHIPLEY.

She was a customer at the store, and the first time I spoke with her—the first time I remember—was when she bought a pressure cooker. I was ringing up the sale when she said, "For the rhubarb."

"For the rhubarb?"

"Oh, did I actually say that out loud? It was running through my mind, and I guess it ran out my mouth, too. I'm sorry."

There was no need to keep the conversation going, but I did. "Now you have to tell me about the rhubarb."

"My grandmother grew it in her garden," she said. "In a shady spot way at the back. Do you know what it looks like?"

"Sort of."

"Deep green leaves and dark red stems. The leaves are supposed to be poisonous."

"Supposed to be?"

"Well," she said, "I can't swear to their toxicity. I never ate one."

"And a good thing, from what I hear."

"And I never knew anyone who ate one, or even heard of anyone who ate one. But all the books warn against eating rhubarb leaves."

"All the books?"

"Not *Peter Rabbit*," she said. "Or *The Power of Positive Thinking*. Or—well, I could go on."

"I imagine you could."

"All the books that mention rhubarb," she said, "warn you about eating the leaves."

"Are there many books that mention rhubarb?"

"Cookbooks. And gardening books. It's very easy to grow."

"And easy to cook?"

"As long as you remember to get rid of the leaves."

"Because they're poisonous."

"Allegedly poisonous," she said. "It's the oxalic acid that makes them dangerous. Of course spinach contains oxalic acid, and beet greens, and swiss chard, and, oh, a good many vegetables."

"Several of which I've eaten," I said. "And lived to tell the tale."

"But no rhubarb leaves?"

"Not a one."

"Wise of you. It's the high concentration of oxalic acid in rhubarb leaves that makes them lethal. If indeed they are."

If there had been a line at the register, the conversation would have long since come to an end. But there was no one within fifty feet of us, and neither of us seemed at a loss for words.

I hefted the pressure cooker, still in its box. The manufacturer was West Bend. I've no idea why I remember that.

"Rhubarb," I said.

"Granny's secret. I assume you've had rhubarb at one time or another."

"Mostly in pie."

"Rhubarb pie."

"And strawberry-rhubarb pie. And once or twice as a side dish."

She nodded. "It's like applesauce," she said, "except it's completely different. One thing, though. It's green."

"While applesauce is—"

"Oh, forget applesauce," she said. "I don't know why I mentioned applesauce. Rhubarb is red when you pick it, or buy it at the market. Green leaves, of course, but forget the leaves."

"Forgotten. Along with the applesauce."

"When you cook rhubarb, it sometimes winds up green. I've no idea why."

"That's interesting."

"No," she said. "It's not, but there's a point to it. My grandmother's rhubarb was always red when she brought it to the table, and can you guess her secret?"

"She made it in a pressure cooker."

Her eyes widened. "How on earth did you know that?"

"Just a lucky guess."

"Well, I'm impressed."

She took her wallet from her purse, counted out bills for the pressure cooker. I said, "Would you like to have dinner with me this evening?"

Did it come out sounding rehearsed? It may well have. I'd been running it through my mind for several minutes, trying out different arrangements of the words.

"I'd love to," she said, without hesitation. Then she said, "Oh, you mean at a restaurant."

"Is that a problem?"

"Not ordinarily," she said, "but my regular sitter is recovering from what I'm not supposed to know is breast enhancement surgery. There are others I could call, but it might be tricky on short notice. Oh!"

"Oh?"

"Come over to my place. That way I won't need a sitter, will I?"

"Probably not."

"I'll cook," she said. "I'll make rhubarb."

SHE DIDN'T MAKE rhubarb. I don't remember what she did make, and didn't really pay all that much attention to the food. I'm sure it was good, because cooking was something she was good at.

Putting me at ease was another.

She was easy to be with, easy to look at, easy to envision as a wife and partner. I don't suppose she was a beautiful woman, not model-beautiful or starlet-pretty, but she was certainly attractive. Looking at her, I felt no urge to fix this or change that. I found her perfectly acceptable just the way she was.

After dinner she poured us glasses of iced tea—neither of us wanted coffee—and we sat on the front porch in straight-backed rocking chairs, sipping our tea. We talked, even as we'd done throughout dinner, and when the conversation eased up we shared the silence. The time when we didn't talk felt oddly more intimate than when we did.

She was thirty-two, the widowed mother of Alden, a nine-year-old boy, who thought he was old enough to stay home alone. "I'm proud of him for thinking so," she said, "but not daft enough to indulge him."

She'd married at twenty-three, given birth at twenty-five. Her husband, three years her senior, had a congenital heart condition that nobody knew about, and died in his sleep less than a month after his son's second birthday.

"I woke up, "she said, "and he didn't."

A rising insurance agent, Duane Shipley had been his own best customer, as members of his profession often were. She received enough money so that she was able to pay off the mortgage on their modest house, because she liked the idea of owning her home free and clear. She put what was left over in a mutual fund and got a dividend check every month. It wasn't a lot, but it helped, and her expenses were low.

And she worked. As a substitute teacher early on, but after she paid for child care she barely came out ahead, and she wanted to be home with her son. So she taught herself book-keeping, let her friends know she was looking for clients, and it wasn't long before she had all the work she wanted.

"And the bookkeeper is the one person who never has to worry about getting paid," she said, "since she's the one who writes the checks."

I told her a little about myself, and most of what I told her was true. A little about my family, a little about my child-hood. I told her I'd had a love affair that ended badly, and it left me just wanting to get away. "So I got in the car and headed east," I said, "and I'd get to a town and find work, but before I was anywhere near settled I'd get the urge for going."

"I always liked that song."

" 'But I never seem to go.' Except as soon as *I* got the urge

I would act on it. Pack my bags, get in my car, and look for the next place."

"Which turned out to be Lima."

"Eventually," I said. "Don't ask me why I stayed here."

"Is it a sensitive subject?"

"No, but it's a question I don't have the answer to. I stuck around, and before I knew it I was settling in and putting down roots. I guess whatever made a nomad out of me used itself up and lost its force. Whatever the explanation, I never did get the urge for going."

"And when you do?"

I took a moment to look at her. "No," I said. "That's not going to happen."

HAD I FALLEN in love?

Hard to say.

When I left her house that night, I did so with the certain knowledge that this was the woman I was going to marry. For a while now I'd been shopping for a wife, but not in any kind of desperate way. The dates I had were auditions of a sort, in that I would imagine each dinner companion as a marriage partner, and knew before the dessert course arrived that the woman across the table from me was not the one.

Louella was entirely different. I was stimulated by her presence, and at the same time I was able to relax in her company. Driving home from her house that first night, I found myself imagining being her husband. Coming home from work, sitting down at the dinner table. Being a father to her son.

I hadn't even met him yet, and I was picturing myself as his father. Alden Shipley—or would I adopt him? He'd never known his father, and if his mother was going to become Louella Thompson, then why shouldn't he be Alden Thompson?

How eager I seemed to be to pass on a name that was not my own in the first place.

AND SO I courted Louella Shipley. Except the verb suggests a campaign which one might seek to win, and looking back I can see that no such campaign was ever required. From that first evening at her house, it was clear to both of us that the future was essentially preordained. By the time I drove away and she headed upstairs to her bed, we had already become a couple.

And yet the courtship proceeded at a measured pace, which is to say that its sexual aspect inched forward in a positively Victorian fashion. And this was not her doing but mine. I don't know that I could have taken her to her bedroom that first night, but it's not inconceivable; we'd bonded, we were taking delight in each other's company, and if I had put an arm around her and given her a kiss and suggested we go upstairs, I'm not sure she would have denied me.

But I can't speak with assurance, because of course I did

no such thing. It was our third or fourth date before I kissed her, and that was not without calculation. We were on her porch, and she was about to go in and pay the babysitter, whom I would then drive home. So we kissed warmly, and I tasted the sweetness of her mouth, and then we had to let go of each other. I waited, and she went into the house, and the designated babysitter, a high school girl liberally dusted with freckles, came out with a backpack slung over her shoulder.

I drove her home, and then drove myself home. And called Louella, to tell her how much I'd enjoyed the evening, and that I'd driven straight home after dropping Jennifer, because I was exhausted and had an early day tomorrow. And made arrangements for us to try a new Mexican restaurant two nights hence.

And so on.

IT SHOULDN'T BE hard to figure out why I was taking my time. Not because I thought it was essential to my long-range purpose. It may be that there are fair ladies who are best won with a faint heart, but Louella was not one of them. She was plainly waiting for me to take her to bed, and even signaled as much when she rested her hand on mine at the dinner table, or gazed at me in a certain way.

What held me back?

Fear, of course. I was afraid. Not of Louella but of myself, of what I might be capable of, of what I already knew myself to be capable of.

Suppose I had the urge to strike her. Suppose my hands, quite of their own accord, found their way around her throat. Suppose everything I did served only to increase my excitement.

Suppose I killed her. Suppose I fucked her dead body.

I had to force myself to think the thoughts, powerless though I was to avoid them. And they turned my stomach.

You are not the man you used to be, I told myself.

An inner voice replied: *The leopard doesn't change its spots.* And so I waited.

WAITING WAS EASY. I'd been waiting for years.

Cindy Raschmann, you see, was the last woman I'd been with.

I suppose that sounds difficult, and unlikely in the bargain. But the last time I'd had sex with a partner, she'd been dead. Dead at my hands. Pure luck had enabled me to get away, and more luck had led me far away from my prior life.

And what a transformation the years had seen! I, who'd been a drifter, had turned myself into a businessman, with a credit rating and money in the bank, with three suits and as many sport jackets in my closet, with memberships in a couple of service clubs and an upscale gym.

I was free and clear now. At worst, the Bakersfield police

would have written off Cindy's murder as a cold case, and one that could only get colder with every passing year. Or they may very well have listed it as solved; men in California do keep on killing women, and now and then one gets caught for it, and who knows how many unsolved murders get conveniently if incorrectly attributed to the son of a bitch? And what could the sorry bastard do about it? *No, no, that's one cunt I never laid a hand on. She's a fucking redhead, right? What kind of a man would fuck a redhead?*

Yeah, right.

So I'd long since ceased worrying that someone with a badge was going to turn up on my doorstep. I wasn't afraid of the Bakersfield cops, or the FBI, or Interpol.

The past was not the problem.

The problem was what might happen . . . if I allowed anything to happen.

The prospect of losing everything—her life, my reinvented life—seemed to me to be a real possibility, and a greater risk than I felt prepared to take. Better to end evenings with a hug and a kiss, and head for home.

STILL, THAT COULD only go on for so long. The embraces, light though they were, stirred me. Back in my own apartment, in my own bed, I'd find myself with thoughts of Louella. Sexual urges rose in me more strongly than they had in longer than I could remember. I found myself imagining her in my arms, in my bed, and I was unwilling to allow myself the fantasies for fear that they would turn violent.

It seems curious, thinking of it now. I was afraid to imagine having sex with Louella for fear of the turns my imagination might take.

Impossible to sustain such a state forever. How long before Louella came to the same conclusion as Myron? He'd assumed I was gay and made a pass. If she made the same assumption . . .

Enough. In the morning, on the way to work, I stopped at a pharmacy and bought a packet of condoms.

DINNER AT HER house. I brought wine. Alden joined us at table, and in front of the television set until his bedtime. Louella went upstairs to tuck him in, and I moved from a chair to the couch, and when she returned she joined me there.

We kissed, held each other. There was a point when she seemed to be on the verge of inviting me upstairs, but she didn't, and I guessed she was afraid I might decline.

And so, at a convenient moment, I told her that she'd never shown me the rest of the house. Something in her face relaxed, and without a word she took my hand and led me to the stairs.

Her body was very nice. She was built, as they say, more for comfort than for speed. Lovely breasts, full hips, just a bit of a belly. I kissed her and stroked her, and I liked the feel of her and the smell of her and the taste of her, and it wasn't long before I was hard and she was wet, and I entered her.

I'd forgotten about the condom, and when I remembered she read my mind before I could draw away. "I'm on the pill," she said.

There was something inexplicably exciting about the way she said that. I fucked her with long probing strokes, slowly at first, then faster and with more urgency, and a sense of surpassing relief came upon me. This was going to be all right after all.

She had an orgasm. My mind slipped off into the past, or perhaps into an alternate present, and I was with some imaginary woman, some fusion of Cindy and Carolyn and God knows who else, and I cried out and came.

AFTERWARD WE WENT downstairs. There must have been six or eight ounces of wine left in the bottle, enough for each of us to have a small glass. I'd dressed and she had put on a robe, and I went home after we'd finished the wine.

In the morning I called a florist and had a dozen red roses delivered. She called to thank me for them, and we agreed she'd call a sitter and we'd have dinner that night. We hurried through dinner, skipped dessert, and went back to my apartment and straight to bed. There was something about the way she was at once properly demure and intensely eager that I found enormously appealing.

I hadn't had sex with anyone but myself in ages. And, in the years before Cindy Raschmann, I'd had little enough of it. What came my way was never really satisfying, and was often made tolerable by fantasies that would have appalled my partners.

I'd never had anything you could call an affair.

And that was what this seemed to be. We settled into a pattern of sorts, saw each other three or four times a week, and neither of us ever stayed over at the other's place. Encounters at my apartment were preceded by a meal or a movie, or a meal *and* a movie. Sometimes she'd have me over for dinner and we'd go upstairs after Alden was asleep; other times we'd dine separately, and I'd drop by after the boy's bedtime.

More than once I was at the point of asking her to marry me. It was clear to me that she was waiting for a proposal, and clear too that she was comfortable enough with waiting. The subject never came up.

What was I waiting for? I'd decided during the rhubarb conversation that this was the woman I would marry. I'd since learned that neither of us bored the other, that our shared silences were as satisfying as our spirited repartee. That I could reveal myself to her—except, of course, for the parts I couldn't reveal.

And more. That she looked good in jeans and a sweater or a skirt and a blouse, and even better without clothes on. What she liked to do in bed, and what she liked done to her.

That one thing she particularly liked about her profession

was the fact that *bookkeeper* was the only word in the English
language with three consecutive pairs of letters, two Os and
two Ks and two Es.

"So far as I know," she said.

AND ONE NIGHT, after we'd been keeping company for
three months or so, I found myself suggesting something new.
"There's something I'd like us to try," I said.

"Oh?"

"You lie perfectly still," I said. "You don't move."

"Like Sleeping Beauty? And you wake me with a kiss?"

"Oh, I kiss you," I said. "And I touch you, and I get on top
of you and inside of you. But you go on sleeping."

"And I can't move?"

"No."

"Like being tied up," she said, "but without the rope."

"And without awareness," I said. "You don't know what's
happening. If you feel anything, you think it's a dream."

"What happens if you make me come?"

"It'll be like coming in your sleep."

She hesitated, and I realized this might not have been such
a good idea. I hadn't preplanned it, the words that came out
of my mouth surprised me almost as much at they surprised
her, and—

I said, "I guess it's not a great idea. It was just a passing
thought."

"I want to do it," she said.

"You don't have to say that."

"No, I mean it. I want to do it. Not that there's anything for me to do. I just lie there?"

I nodded, and she closed her eyes. And waited for me to do whatever I wanted to do.

AND SO SHE lay still, as still as easeful death, while I had my way with her. My way and her way, because I did all the things I'd learned to do to and for her.

I was excited at first, excited by her deliberate mimicry of unconsciousness—and her unwitting mimicry of death. But then I felt horribly self-conscious, and realized that this was not going to work, that it would fail and might take our budding relationship down with it. I fancied I could feel her observing me, judging me.

And then, while I was using my mouth on her, something shifted.

She was becoming excited.

I knew this, but knew it in the absence of evidence. She remained still, motionless. Perhaps there was a slight change in her breathing, but perhaps not. It was not her behavior but her energy that changed, and I was aware of it without being able to define it.

Something let go within me, some knot in some

metaphorical muscle found a way to untie itself. A fog lifted, a cloud dispersed. What I was doing took me over utterly.

And now, much to my own surprise, I feel the need to draw a curtain. When I sit down to my task as Recording Devil, the words come in a stream, as if my psyche has had its daily dose of Flo-Max. I've been able to write, without much effort and little inhibition, about my deepest and most insupportable secrets, and to do so in unwholesome detail.

But to describe my adventure with Louella seems beyond me. I've been groping for words, stumbling over phrases, and deleting one sentence after another.

Just write it, I tell myself. Just put the words down. You can come back and fix it later.

Instead I keep backspacing, erasing, trying again. There would seem to be some realm of privacy, mine or hers, that I am not prepared to invade.

And, you know, I don't have forever. Thus the curtain.

"OH MY DARLING. How did you even think of that? And how did you know I would love it?"

"And did you?"

"I didn't even come. Not exactly. It was like coming, but it wasn't my body that did it. Does that make any sense?"

"I think I know what you mean."

"And what *I* think is I would have come if I hadn't held myself back. This time it was nice letting a part of me just sit in the audience. You know, observing. Next time—oh!"

"What?"

"Well, maybe you won't want to do it like this again. But you enjoyed it, didn't you?"

"Couldn't you tell?"

"I just wanted to be sure."

AND, A DAY or two later: "Oh, I'm just so sleepy. Look at me, I'm yawning, I can't keep my eyes open. I know it's early, but would it be all right if I went to bed?"

"That sounds like a good idea to me."

"So tired. I'll just drop my clothes on the chair here, because I'm too tired to hang them up. I just know I'll be out cold the second my head hits the pillow."

I'd wondered if novelty had been what made our first game of Sleeping Beauty so thrilling, for her and for me. And that may have engendered some of the excitement, but this second go-round, unburdened by performance anxiety, was in fact everything the first time had been, and more.

This time I could feel her holding herself in check as she approached orgasm, and I held back myself until I couldn't.

I cried out, and that set her off and let her drop the reins and give her body its reward.

AFTERWARD, OVER CUPS of decaf, I told her I thought we ought to get married.

"Oh, my darling," she said. "I think we already are."

AND SO WE lived happily ever after.

It took me forever to type that sentence. Not to hit the right keys in the proper sequence, that was quick and simple enough. But to hear the words in my mind, and see them in my mind's eye, and finally to will my fingers to tap the keys.

And, having at last managed to perform the action, I sat for the longest time looking at the seven words upon the screen. Read them over and over.

Highlighted them, so that I might delete them with a single keystroke. Moved the cursor, clicked, and let them be as they were.

And shut down the computer for the day.

It has been my habit, since I began this project-for-which-I-do-not-have-a-name, to sit down daily at the computer and say what I have to say. If I've missed my daily stint, it's been because I simply forgot, or was just too busy to spare the time.

Now, for the first time, I consciously chose to stay away from my laptop.

Which is not to say I stopped thinking about it. Quite the reverse.

Was my work complete, my prose composition at its natural conclusion? "And so we lived happily ever after"—was that the perfect way to end it? It was, after all, the traditional way one ended a story told to a child.

Or at least it used to be. But I'm not sure today's children believe in happy endings.

No, leaving the laptop unopened didn't stop the parade of thoughts. For three days they ran in my mind, and now I'm here again, my fingers on the keys.

Because it's become all too evident that the only way to clear my mind is to dump its contents on the screen.

SO: WE LIVED HAPPILY.

The wedding was small and simple. Some years ago I'd become a congregant at a Presbyterian church, much as I'd joined Rotary and Kiwanis and the Lions. One got along better if one belonged. But I maintained my membership by writing checks a couple of times a year, and that was rather more frequently than I attended a Sunday service.

Louella had been brought up in a Protestant denomination, I don't recall which one, but Duane Shipley had been an ex-Catholic turned atheist. He'd become bitterly anticlerical, and she suspected some robed pedophile might have been to blame for his transformation. Whatever its origins, he'd insisted on a nonreligious ceremony at city hall, and that was fine with her.

After she was widowed, she'd let one or another girlfriend drag her to a Sunday service, but such visits never led anywhere. There was a time when a neighbor with a child Alden's age asked Louella if she'd allow Alden to visit their Sunday school, and he tagged along dutifully on three successive Sundays.

She asked if he liked it. "Not much," he said, and was relieved when she said he didn't have to go anymore.

I knew a county judge who would marry us, but I thought I might as well get some return on the checks I'd been writing over the years, and asked Louella if a Presbyterian wedding would suit her. She liked the idea, and we met with the minister and planned a small ceremony.

The only relative with whom she had any contact was her older sister, Marian, who'd gone to Indiana State University. She'd stayed on after graduation, moved away periodically to Colorado and California, but always sooner or later returned to Terre Haute. The sisters exchanged cards at Christmas, and a couple of times a year Louella would get a middle-of-the-night phone call from Marian.

I'd been on hand for one. We were in Louella's bedroom and she'd just turned off the light when the phone rang. I left the room to give her some privacy, and when I came back she said it was Marian, which I'd gathered, and that she sounded like she'd been drinking, which I'd suspected.

Now it was Louella, who hadn't been drinking, who called Marian, to invite her to serve as matron of honor. "She was all excited," she reported, "and quick to correct me. Bridesmaid, not matron of honor, because she's single again. I wonder what it'll be like to see her. Terre Haute's what, a four-hour drive? She drove up for Duane's funeral, but she hasn't made the trip since."

"And you haven't been to Terre Haute."

"I've never been to Terre Haute. The only reason to go there would be to see Marian, and somehow that's never been enough of a reason. She's all the family I've got, and two or three times a year she has a couple of drinks and picks up the phone, and if she didn't we'd lose touch altogether. And your family—"

I'd grown up in foster care, I'd told her, and invented a pair of foster parents who'd been stern and distant. They'd been past fifty when they took me in, I said, and were almost certainly gone by now.

She looked at me. "We'll be a family," she said.

AND INDEED WE were. After a few months I'd bonded with

Alden sufficiently for me to take him aside and ask him how he felt about my adopting him. I told him he could take his time and think about it, and he responded by throwing his arms around me. And so I would become his father, and he would cease to be Alden Shipley, a name of some distinction and one he'd come by honestly, and would replace it with the surname of Thompson, which was neither distinctive nor legitimate.

"Alden Wade Thompson," he said, trying the name on his tongue. He nodded solemnly, evidently happy enough with the name, but something in his tone gave me an idea.

"You know," I said, "your first father was a good man, and he had a good name. Maybe you'd want to keep it as a middle name."

"And get rid of Wade?"

"There's no reason why a man can't have more than one middle name. Do you remember who invented the telegraph?"

He supplied the answer-question we'd heard just days ago on *Jeopardy*: " 'Who was Samuel F.B. Morse?' What do the F and B stand for?"

Google answered the question for him.

"Samuel Finley Breese Morse," he reported. "Alden Wade Shipley Thompson. Wade Shipley? Or Shipley Wade?"

"I think Wade Shipley."

"Alden Wade Shipley Thompson," he said, and at the dinner table that evening he said it again, and met his mother's eyes. "Well? What do you think?"

"I think it's a shame somebody already invented the

telegraph," she said, "but I'm sure you'll find an even more impressive way to bring honor to your name."

"By inventing something?" He thought about it. "You know what would be great? A fax machine for people. You get in the chamber and throw a switch and the next thing you know you're in Cincinnati."

HE SEEMED HAPPY to have a father. Even as I found myself happy to have a son.

And, not quite two years later, a daughter.

"A girl," Louella said, when the ultrasound had so informed us. "A baby sister for Alden. A daughter for you."

"And for you."

"Yes, for me. You know I'd have been happy enough with another boy. A blessing is a blessing. But oh, won't it be wonderful to have a little girl?"

And, almost in the next breath: "But all of a sudden I'm so tired, darling. I should be ashamed of myself, but I can't keep my eyes open. How awful would it be if I took off all these clothes and just dropped off into a deep sleep?"

SO THERE WERE four of us, Louella and Alden and Kristin and I. By then we were in a four-bedroom older home on a good street. It was convenient to Alden's school and almost as close to what would be his high school, and no more than a twenty-minute walk from the store.

Thompson Dawes Hardware. I'd kept Porter Dawes's name on the business after his death, as much out of inertia as respect, and it wasn't until Louella and I were keeping company that I added my own. She'd begun serving as my book-keeper—two o's, two k's, two e's—and wondered why I didn't have my own name on the store.

I said that everybody knew Dawes Hardware, and she said most of them knew John Thompson owned and operated it, and for the price of a new sign I could share the glory with the late Mr. Dawes. And it would be a good excuse for a sale, and that would more than cover the signage expense.

"And Porter Dawes doesn't mean anything to anybody in Penderville, and calling the new store Dawes Hardware would just have them scratching their heads. Which is prob-ably the local sport anyway in Penderville, but never mind. But if you called both stores Thompson Dawes Hardware—"

"Home Depot would be green with envy," I said. "Thomp-son & Dawes?"

"I think just Thompson Dawes. But with or without a hy-phen?" She picked up a pencil, wrote down both versions. "I think no hyphen," she said.

The original store was not quite a mile from the new house, and on nice days I walked there more often than not. The Penderville store proved profitable from the start, and as part of his silent partnership, Ewell Kennerly had recom-mended a Penderville nephew of his as manager. I suppose that fit the dictionary definition of nepotism, but in this instance it proved good policy, and the new store pretty much ran itself. I drove over there once a week, had a proprietary look around, enjoyed coffee and conversation with Ewell's nephew, made whatever executive decisions I was called upon to make, and resisted the temptation to look for other opportunities to expand. I was happy with the second store, but that was plenty.

Happy with the house, too. It suited us from the day we moved in, and didn't require much in the way of improvements. A new kitchen, some remodeling in two of the bathrooms. The backyard garden had well-established shrubs and perennials, and required nothing more than weeding and pruning.

Thompson Dawes supplied what tools we needed. And the paint, when we spruced up the front porch. And whatever else was required when, not long after his fourteenth birthday, Alden suggested we finish the third-floor attic. Insulation would pay for itself by cutting heating costs, he pointed out, and if we carved out a bedroom for him up there he could play his music without disturbing the rest of us.

"And my old room could be a second home office," he said, "or, I don't know, a TV room or something? And, you know, if we did the work upstairs ourselves—"

"It might be fun?"

"Plus we'd develop new skills we could use later on."

I'm not sure what new skills we developed, or how likely it was that we'd find further use for them. But it was indeed enjoyable, although it turned out to be more work than we'd anticipated. Alden's initial proposal hadn't included a third-floor bathroom, but Louella pointed out the wisdom of adding one, and that meant bringing in a plumber and getting some professional help with designing the addition.

"Everything is more work than you think," I told Alden, "and takes longer than planned, and costs more than you estimated."

He nodded, and I could see him filing the statement away as something to be remembered.

It's one day short of a week since I got anything written. I found reasons to take two days off. Then I came in here, sat down, opened the file, and immediately thought of a question Google could answer for me. I bounced around the internet for an hour or two, fascinated by subjects that would have been far less fascinating on another day, then logged off and closed the laptop's lid.

Then there was a day spent reading what I'd written, something I'd previously avoided doing, and apparently for good cause. It left me in an anxious state, so I wrote nothing that day. Or the day after, when I sat down, opened the file to where I'd left off, wrote and rewrote a sentence only to erase it. When I ultimately gave up, the document—or whatever I might want to call this collection of pixels—was as I'd found it hours earlier.

And as I find it now, but for the addition of these italicized paragraphs, which are not writing so much as they're writing about writing.

It's not hard to fathom why I don't want to go on.

We were happy then, and it seems to me that what I've written does a good job of conveying that happiness. Why mar it with intimations of what's to come?

Because in truth we're happy now. The four of us—or five, really, because why leave out the dog? Chester, part of our family for close to three years now, a good-sized dog of undetermined ancestry who'd followed Kristin home from school one day.

No tags, no collar, nothing to indicate where he'd come from or who might miss him. His tail never stopped wagging, as if to dismiss out of hand any notion of taking him to the pound. A vet pronounced him free of any identifying chips or tags, and free too of any disqualifying ailments. "Around three years old, John. He won't get any larger, although he might fill out some if you feed him right. As for who his parents might be, well, I think I can see some shepherd in there, but beyond that I'd say your guess is as good as mine."

We ran an ad—DOG FOUND—but pulled it after two days when we realized how anxious we all got whenever the phone rang. Whoever had lost him—or, more likely, abandoned him—either never saw the ad or felt no compulsion to respond to it.

So we bought him a proper collar and a leash and dog dish and a drinking bowl, and the vet fitted him with an ID microchip, and Louella filled out a form and paid his license fee.

He already had a name. Kristin, who'd brought him home,

had taken to calling him Chester. No one knew why, but no one had objected, least of all the dog himself. His ears perked up whenever he heard his name, and he came trotting over to get his head patted.

If there were ever any question that we were a family, Chester settled it. He was indisputably a family dog, and how could you have a family dog if you weren't a family?

He was also the beginning of the end, although you couldn't really blame him for it.

"DAD, I WAS THINKING."

"A hazardous occupation," I said. "But not without its occasional rewards."

"Huh? Oh, right. No, what I was thinking about was college. And like after."

"Oh?"

"Like, you know, what do I want to do with my life."

"Deep thoughts."

He nodded, made air quotes. "Deep thoughts. And what part of me wants to do is four years in Athens at OU and then come back to Thompson Dawes."

He'd been helping out after school, working in the stockroom, waiting on customers, making himself generally useful. I'd always had it in mind that he or his sister would most likely take over the business when I was ready to let it go.

I said, "Part of you. And what about the other part?"

"Well, I was thinking."

This time I was the one who made air quotes.

"Right," he said. "Deep thoughts. What I was thinking, I was thinking about becoming a vet."

My first thought was he wanted to enlist in the service, because how else did you become a veteran? Then he said something about how he'd been getting to know Ralph Debenthal, from taking Chester in for booster shots and general maintenance, and—

"Oh, for God's sake. A veterinarian."

"You think it's a bad idea?"

"I think it's a lot better idea than the infantry. You said 'vet' and I figured you were all set to enlist in the army."

"Me?"

"Well, it wasn't what I was expecting."

"God, I hope not. No, I thought it might be good to do what Doctor Ralph does."

"A vet rather than—"

"A people doctor, but there must be a better word for it. A physician?"

"That's the word."

"I thought of that. When Mom was sick."

Breast cancer, caught in its early stages, well in advance of metastasis. She'd had a lumpectomy and a brief course of radiation, and was now cancer-free. And there was no reason to fear a recurrence.

Except, of course, that there always is. There is, in this swamp of human existence, an unending abundance of crocodiles.

"But med school's such a slog," he said. "That's what everybody says. It's tough to get in and tough to get through it, and then you're an intern and they work you like twenty hours a day."

"It does require a commitment."

"And that might even be okay, if I had my heart set on it, but it's easier for me to see myself giving rabies shots than telling people Grandma's not going to get better so start planning the funeral. I told Sukie I was thinking about vet school, and she said why not med school, and I said I like animals better than people."

"And well you might."

"I was just being, you know, I guess the word is glib."

"But there's some truth in it."

"Yeah, there is. They don't judge you or sue you for malpractice. Although I guess their owners might."

"Not that often."

"No. Anyway, it's nothing I need to decide, but—"

I said, "You might want to think about shadowing Ralph."

"What, like a detective? Skulking around?"

NOT LIKE A detective, and not furtively. He told Ralph Debenthal of his interest, and they agreed he could come in two days a week after school, running errands and performing menial tasks while seeing what Ralph did and how he did it. The man himself was reserved and laconic, and it was not hard to believe that he felt more comfortable with animals than human beings, but he got used to Alden's company and increasingly opened up to him.

Then one evening just before dinner, Alden called Chester to his side, ordered him to sit, and placed a hand on top of the dog's head. "Ah, I'm picking up information," he announced. "About your ancestry, Chester." He scanned the room, eyed each of us in turn. "A shepherd mix," he said. "Isn't that what we've been telling ourselves?"

Kristin asked him what he was talking about.

"I'm talking about Chester," he said, "who is indeed about a quarter shepherd, but Belgian shepherd, not German. But what old Chester is more than anything else is Rottweiler. He's fifty percent Rottie, so the odds are pretty good that either his mother or his father was a purebred Rottweiler."

And how did he know this? "Oh, I have my ways," he said, and waited to be coaxed into a full explanation—how there was this company in Fort Smith, Arkansas, that offered a full genetic profile of your dog for under a hundred dollars. What you did, you sent them a check—or in his case a money order, purchased with his own funds at the branch post office on Elizabeth Street. They mailed you a kit, and you took each of the two oversized Q-tips and swabbed the inside of your dog's cheek. You put them in individual plastic tubes, used the company's pre-addressed mailer, and sent it all back. And then you sat around waiting, and by the time you'd pretty much forgotten the whole thing, they sent you a letter with the results.

And those results, which he'd just received that afternoon,

were pretty clear-cut. Half Rottweiler, around a quarter Belgian shepherd, and the remainder a little harder to pin down.

He beamed. Chester wagged his tail.

IN NOVEMBER OF 1942, two years and four months before I was born, Winston Churchill delivered a speech at a luncheon at London's Mansion House. In Egypt, Generals Alexander and Montgomery had routed Rommel's forces at El Alamein, providing Churchill for the first time with a victory to celebrate.

"Now this is not the end," he said. "It is not even the beginning of the end. But it is, perhaps, the end of the beginning."

I'd come across this once, years ago, but looked it up now to get it right. I typed "Churchill the end of the beginning" and Google supplied the precise quotation, along with more information on the occasion than I needed to know. I found it interesting enough to read in full, perhaps to keep my mind from going where it would have to go next.

The end of the beginning.

NONE OF THAT occurred to me at the time. I was at least as proud of Alden as he was of himself—that he'd thought of investigating the dog's ancestry, and that he'd carried it off without dropping a hint until he had the results in hand. I was probably less surprised by his resourcefulness than by Chester's heritage; the name Rottweiler conjured up images of a heavily-built, powerful beast, its jaws fastened in a death grip on any perceived threat to the family it was there to protect. That seemed a stretch for our Chester, who was more an affable clown, but they do say blood will tell, and I suppose so will DNA.

Ah yes. DNA.

THE MOLECULE NOW known as DNA was first identified in the 1860s by a Swiss chemist called Johann Friedrich Miescher. You probably didn't know that, and neither did I until I Googled my way to it a few minutes ago.

It was almost a century later, in 1953, when James Watson and Francis Crick discovered the double helix structure of DNA, and in the decades that followed the world has been working out what to make of it—and what to do with it.

It took a mere fifteen years to get to 1968, that pivotal year in which death came to a remarkable roster of people whose names you'll know. John Steinbeck, Helen Keller, Yuri Gagarin. Tallulah Bankhead, Edna Ferber. Upton Sinclair. Norman Thomas. Martin Luther King.

Let's not forget Bobby Kennedy. And, linked to him in my mind if in no one else's, Cindy Raschmann.

IN 1968 A MAN walked into a bar, and while he must have heard the iconic initials of deoxyribonucleic acid they'd made no impression upon him. The man in the *Buddy* shirt paid little attention to the news in general and less to that of scientific advances and Nobel prizes.

Indeed, I'd have needed to be more than attentive to attach much significance to DNA. Uncommon prescience would have been required for me or anyone else to realize the eventual implications of Watson and Crick's discovery.

Had I been gifted with that sort of foresight, I might have put on a condom before I took my pleasure with the late Cindy Raschmann.

But why? There were at that time just two reasons to don that sheer armor, and neither led me even to consider so doing. The prevention of conception was one, protection from disease the other.

I hadn't needed to be concerned about birth control, as no man, however virile, was likely to get a dead girl pregnant. I suppose one might as readily pick up syphilis or gonorrhea from a dead partner as a living one, but I never gave a thought to VD back then. It was reputed to be no worse than a bad cold, and more fun to catch, and one simple shot of penicillin cured it, and you wouldn't wear a raincoat in the shower, would you? Or wash your feet with your socks on?

Now, of course, nobody says VD. It's STD now. I'm not

sure why *Sexually Transmitted Disease* should better characterize those complaints we used to categorize as *Venereal Disease*, but then I've never been able to work out why the phrase *person of color* is preferable to *colored person*.

For whatever reason, STD is all you hear nowadays. And there seem to be more of them than there used to be, and many have become largely resistant to penicillin and its cousins. Some are a good deal worse than a bad cold; for a decade or two, one of them—AIDS—killed everyone who came down with it. It's still incurable, but its victims are now able to go on living with it, year after year, and perhaps they tell each other it's no worse than the heartbreak of psoriasis. And, I suppose, more fun to catch.

So easy for me to go on like this. So effortless to let one's fingers on the keys record the wandering of one's mind. Such satisfaction in highlighting a word that's almost right and replacing it with one that's better.

So much easier than pushing aside the trivial and getting on with it.

> *The Moving Finger writes; and, having writ,*
> *Moves on: nor all thy Piety nor Wit*
> *Shall lure it back to cancel half a Line*
> *Nor all thy Tears wash out a Word of it.*

I wouldn't punctuate it that way, or single out those seven words for capitalization, and indeed I wasted a quarter of an hour nattering on about the subject before I used the Delete key for its intended purpose.

Cut the crap, Buddy. Get on with it.

I DON'T KNOW when some forensic trailblazer thought of using DNA as a forensic tool, nor could I tell you when I first became aware of it. But it became increasingly evident that the substance could snare you if you were guilty or exonerate you if you were innocent. Prison cell doors sprang open, abruptly releasing men who'd long since given up all hope of ever walking free. And then these doors slammed shut again, confining for the rest of their lives men who'd come to take their continuing freedom for granted.

Men whose circumstances were not unlike those of that Ohio shopkeeper known as John James Thompson.

I had gotten away with what I'd done to Cindy Raschmann. By the time I walked into that bar, I'd lived my life without drawing any attention from the police, outside of a couple of traffic stops. I'd never been arrested, never been fingerprinted. I couldn't see how I might have left fingerprints at the crime scene, but even if I had, and even if some enterprising crime scene investigator succeeded in raising them, they wouldn't lead anywhere.

But I'd pumped her full of DNA, hadn't I? I'd left genetic fingerprints, and with the passage of time and the refinement of technology, I began to see what that might mean.

Of course, it might mean nothing at all. Who was to say how extensive Cindy's post-mortem examination might have been, or what they might have kept of what they'd found? She'd never had a chance to claw at me, so there'd be none of my DNA under her fingernails, but if they'd retained what they found of my semen, and if it hadn't been lost over the years, or degraded to be rendered forensically useless, then it might be enough to let them catch up with me.

If I somehow became a suspect. If I drew their attention. If they picked me up, and swabbed my cheek, and extracted the telltale DNA from my epithelial cells—if that happened, they'd have hard scientific evidence that would stand up in court, where some acknowledged expert could estimate the odds of another person's DNA matching mine at one in a billion or a trillion or a quadrillion.

But first they had to arrest me before they could swab my cheek, and before that they'd have to suspect me, and why should they even know of the existence of J. J. Thompson, the mild-mannered proprietor of Thompson Dawes? Why should my new life call me to their attention?

I was still very much in the clear, wasn't I?

WELL, LESS SO as time passed. The establishment of a DNA data bank came to mean that anyone who'd been arrested and cheek-swabbed was to be found in that system. If I walked into another bar, in Ohio or California or anywhere else in the country, and if I did what I'd once done to Cindy Ra-schmann, and if I were caught in the act or tracked down after it, some cold case investigator in Bakersfield could find a match for the sample he'd had in storage all these years.

If they'd had it to begin with, and hadn't lost it, or—

Never mind. Technology marched on, and from a certain distance I found myself keeping up with it. I didn't watch the original *CSI*, the one set in Las Vegas, because it aired on my bowling night, but it came up enough in dinner-table conversation for me to be aware of it. And when they put on the spinoff shows, set in Miami and New York, Louella and I would watch, joined as often as not by Alden.

Even before that, if we were home on a Saturday night we were apt to be watching *America's Most Wanted*. Early on I'd catch myself on edge at the prospect that Cindy Raschmann's 1968 death would turn up on the screen. Some passing motorist might come forward years later, recalling a partial license plate. A roadhouse patron might happen to remember a man in work clothes, the embroidery on his shirt identifying him as *Buddy*.

And then one Saturday her picture flashed on the screen.

I doubt I'd have recognized it if they hadn't said her name. It must have been her high school yearbook photograph, and she'd lived some years and had some hard mileage on her by the time our paths crossed. I had time to note that she looked oddly familiar, and then I heard her name, and half-expected to hear mine coupled with it. My original name, that is to say. They wouldn't be likely to know the Thompson name.

If they did, there'd have already been a knock on my door.

But what they had didn't lead to me, and didn't really lead to Cindy Raschmann, either. Here's what they had: A bespectacled middle-aged man who'd sold used cars all over the Pacific seaboard, and who looked for all the world like an accountant, had been in a bar in Eugene, Oregon, when a fight broke out, and the police dragged everybody down to the stationhouse.

I forget what the evidentiary link was, even as I forget the fellow's name, but he broke down under questioning and admitted to the recent rape of a college student, and went on to confess to several more rapes, a couple of which had ended in the victim's death.

So now police departments throughout the region were looking at him as a suspect in whatever cold cases matched his profile. Cindy Raschmann's murder was one such case, and her name and picture one that made it to the broadcast. Bakersfield police had been optimistic he'd turn out to be their guy, we were told, but the timeline didn't work. And, they added, there was physical evidence that excluded him.

I had a moment when my optimism matched that of the Bakersfield cops. They wouldn't have to build a solid case against the car salesman. All they needed was reason to believe he'd done it. Oregon could prosecute for crimes he'd clearly committed, and Bakersfield, on their own, could decide he was Cindy's killer and close their very cold case.

But that wasn't to be. And, sitting in front of the TV, I sorted the good and bad news. The good news, along with the fact that this particular menace would be off the streets for the rest of his life, was that I was no closer to drawing the attention of the authorities.

The bad news? That the case, however cold, was still open.

And that they had physical evidence. If it was sufficient to exclude the car salesman, one had to presume it would serve to include the guy in the *Buddy* shirt. The man who'd actually

"done the deed." That's how I'd have finished that thought. I had it in mind when I stopped writing yesterday, stopping in the middle of a sentence as I've occasionally done so that I'll know where to pick up the next day. Or a few days down the line, if it takes me that long to get back to this curious task I've set myself.

I have to interrupt myself, I have to dart ahead into present time. Because I had a visitor last night. And no, it was not the one I'd been dreading, the faceless fellow in uniform knocking on my front door.

It was Cindy Raschmann.

Know that I was asleep, stretched out on my back on the left-hand side of the marital bed, with Louella sound asleep next to me.

"Oh, the old fool had a dream."

That's what you'd have to think, isn't it? But Cindy Raschmann has invaded my dreams from time to time over the years, insinuating herself into an appropriate or inappropriate portion of a dream's haphazard narrative. I don't often remember the specifics of such visits, typically recalling only that she was there. Or some anonymous dream character turns around, and

her face is Cindy's. Or I pick up a newspaper, and the headlines are unreadable, but there's a picture and I can see that
it's her.

Or—oh, never mind. Those are dreams. I can summon up
wispy memories of some of them, consisting perhaps of nothing more than the dim recollection that she was present. And
in fact I may have seen that face a thousand more times in
dreams of which I never became consciously aware.

Dreams. They are, as best I understand it, how the mind at
rest sorts through and processes elements with which it is not
entirely at ease. Aren't there experiments in which subjects pre-
vented from dreaming are rendered mentally and emotionally
fragile in their waking hours?

Last night was different.

I was asleep in bed, and I was conscious of a presence, and
without knowing who it was I was nevertheless afraid to open
my eyes and see for myself. But then I did, and there she was,
and I recognized her instantly.

She was wearing the scoop-necked blouse, the skintight
jeans, the boots. She was older, but not as old she she'd have
been if she lived. Say late forties, early fifties, as if she'd aged a
single year for every two in real time.

I'm thinking that now. At the time all I could think was
that this was Cindy Raschmann, this was the woman I'd
killed. In my house, in my bedroom, standing at the foot of
my bed.

Her vivid blue eyes were quickly locked with mine.

Her eyes, her eyes. I half-remembered them as blue, but I

couldn't have sworn to their color, although I never failed to recall watching the light go out of them. In memory they always
presented themselves as oddly colorless, virtual blank circles.
Little Orphan Annie Eyes, wide with something. Dread or
wonder, I suppose.

"Hey, it's Buddy," she said.

Her first words to me all those years ago. Then she'd been
squinting at my pocket, working to bring the embroidered letters into focus. Now her brow was unlined, her blue eyes aimed
not at my breast but at my own blue eyes.

Not so blue as hers, though. The years had washed some of
the color out of mine, even as they'd turned my hair gray.

The years do take their toll . . .

Hey, it's Buddy. The words echoed in the bedroom's silence. I parted my lips to reply but couldn't find words of my
own.

Nor did she seem to be waiting for me to say anything. She
just went on gazing into my eyes, and I into hers.

Then she said, "You've been waiting such a long time, have-
n't you? Except there is no time, you know. Time was created
to keep everything from happening at once. But it doesn't really work, because everything really does happen all at once."

I was conscious of two things at once—that her words didn't
make any sense, and that I somehow understood them and
found them brilliant.

She fell silent, and I remained unable to speak, and our blue
eyes, hers and mine, maintained their unbreakable connection.
Something passed between us, almost electrical in nature, but
whatever it was seemed to be beyond words, beyond thought.

No idea how long this took. But if there was no time, who can put a number to it?

"I forgive you."

Three words, spoken with—as best I recall—no inflection whatsoever. A rush of indefinable feeling overwhelmed me. There was something I needed to say and I had no idea what it was. I opened my mouth to let the words out, but there were no words there, nothing for me to say, and as I came to grips with that realization, she began to evanesce.

I think that's the word I want. I first typed "disappear," but it doesn't seem to me to convey what I observed. Her image somehow lost substance, or lost the appearance of substance, growing pale and, well, immaterial. I can't seem to render this accurately, perhaps because I don't really know what I saw, or didn't see.

I don't know how long the process took. In her timeless universe, I suppose it took no time at all. In mine, it took somewhere between no time at all and all the time in the world.

Oh, never mind. She was there, vividly, and then she was less and less present, and then she was gone.

Where she'd been I now saw not the normal view from where I lay, not my chest of drawers and Louella's dressing table and the entrance to the en suite bathroom, but an open vista. Western, from the looks of it, with mountains rising far in the distance.

How could that be? How could I be lying in bed with my eyes open and gazing at a setting that, if it existed at all, was at least a thousand miles from where I lay?

I blinked, and what I saw was unchanged. I willed my eyes shut, and kept them shut, and my vision remained unaltered—that vast expanse of open land, then foothills, then faraway mountain peaks.

Eyes open, eyes shut. No change.

How could that be?

My mind struggled to come to grips with what it knew, or seemed to know. Here I was, with my eyes wide open, and how could that be?

"With my eyes wide open I'm dreaming . . ." A line from a song, although it came to me then with no melody to carry it.

But were they open?

I managed to figure out, or was somehow given to know, that they were not. I was in fact not sitting up but lying on my back as I always did when I slept, and my eyes were closed.

It was not without effort that I willed them open, not the eyes that had opened to engage Cindy's blue eyes but my own physical eyes. I'm struggling to explain this, but it's a fool's errand, for how can I explain what I don't myself understand?

Here's what I do understand, or at least what I recall. I was in fact lying in my bed, conscious of the presence beside me of my sleeping wife. There was no great vista, no distant mountains, just the usual quotidian backdrop of a maple chest of drawers and a dressing table.

My heart, while not exactly racing, was beating a little more rapidly than usual.

I closed my eyes—actually closed their lids—and settled my head on my pillow. You'll never get back to sleep, I told myself, and the next thing I knew it was morning.

I've thought about this. Oh, it was a dream . . . *except I don't think that's the word for it. It was all still vividly there in memory when I finally opened my eyes to a bright morning. Indeed, it's here now. Dreams, when I'm conscious of having had them, are quickly dispersed by the light of dawn. But this experience of mine is no less real now than it was a few hours ago.*

Google proved helpful, as it so often does, leading me to discover that there was a distinction to be drawn between the dream state and the experience I'd undergone, for which the term seemed to be visitation. *I followed the word down the internet rabbit hole and saw it all become at once clearer and more confusing.*

Apparently the woman I saw was real, and not a figment of my imagination. She had no conventional corporeal reality, she'd proved that by dispersing like fog in morning sunlight; she'd left no footprints on the bedroom carpet, and had there been a tape recorder running, it would not have picked up the words she said.

So was I then visited by her disembodied spirit? Were people survived by such spirits, and could they turn up in one's bed-chamber after such a span of time? Yes, it was true that she'd said (or I'd sensed her to be saying) that there was no time, that in the sphere in which she existed everything essentially

*happened at once. But in my universe, in the sphere in which
I exist, there is indeed such a thing as time, and a considerable
amount of it had unspooled between our two meetings.*

Why had I received this visitation now?

*And whose idea had it been? Even if it were not a dream
but a visitation, even if an existing spirit had come from its
own reality into mine, was this in part my doing? Had something in my own mind made this happen, not by spinning it
into a dream but by summoning that surviving unmurdered
part of her to stand at the foot of my bed?*

*I couldn't answer these questions. I could barely wrap my
mind around them sufficiently to ask them. I might as well
have tried to call back the spirit who'd come to me, or to slip
back into the unreal reality of a dream.*

*Two questions lingered: Why now? Followed in due course
by Now what?*

"DAD?"

I was at Thompson Dawes, in the little office in back, seated at my desk. The oak desk and the matching swivel chair
had been there when Porter Dawes owned the place; they'd
outlasted him and would likely outlast me as well. Some years
back I'd replaced one of the chair's casters, and one of the
desk drawers could be difficult to open on humid days, but
age had been kinder to them than it is to most of us.

"Dad, I figured out what I want to get you for Christmas, and it can only partly be a surprise."

I don't know that the discovery of his genetic makeup meant a great deal to Chester. He was the same creature, whether or not we knew he was half-Rottweiler, and I don't think any of us related to him any differently for the knowledge.

But it changed Alden's life. He was now spending not two but four afternoons a week at the Debenthal Small Animal Clinic, and Ralph was paying him for his time.

He still ran errands, and observed procedures. But he also swabbed cheeks, because the good Doctor Debenthal had been interested to learn about Chester's DNA results—he'd never have guessed Rottweiler, he said, not in a million dog years. He might have taken it the next step and thought of offering DNA testing to his patients, but it was Alden who suggested it, and Ralph to his credit who saw at once the merits of the suggestion.

There was, one or the other of them would tell a customer, this online service that could tell you all about Towser's ancestry. They send you a kit and all you had to do was reach into his mouth and swab his cheeks and mail in the specimens, and they get back to you with the results. *Or we can take care of all of that for you, and I'll do it right now, if you'd like.*

"Almost everybody goes for it," Alden told me.

It was a good profit center for Ralph, and he responded by finding more things for Alden to do—and putting him on the payroll.

"It'll only take a minute," he told me now, "and it's totally pain-free."

He brandished a pair of oversized cotton swabs. I think I must have been half-waiting for this, albeit unconsciously, but still it took me by surprise, and not in a good way. And I guess this showed in my face.

"No pain," he assured me. "All you have to do is open your mouth. Or take the swabs and do it yourself."

I said, "I don't think so, Alden."

"Seriously? Because I thought, you know, here's a perfect present for you. You said you don't know anything about where your grandparents came from—"

"They were all born in America," I said.

"As far as you know."

"Right."

"But what about your great-grandparents, or even going back generations? They'd have to be from someplace else. Unless some of them were Indians, and wouldn't that be cool? I mean maybe you'd turn out to be part Choctaw or Apache or Pawnee, whatever, and you could, I don't know, open a casino or something?"

How to say this? How to explain without explaining?

"If I'm part Rottweiler," I said, "I'd be just as happy not knowing it."

"But why, Dad? Aren't you even a little bit curious?"

"My childhood," I said, "was not a happy time."

"You said you had foster parents."

"That's right."

"And growing up in foster care wasn't so great."

"It wasn't."

"And you barely remember your real parents."

Was that how I'd put it? "I remember a little," I said. "I remember more than I want to."

"Oh?"

"I've worked hard to keep those memories from surfacing. In fact I've done what I can to avoid remembering those early years, and the last thing I want is to know more about the people I've been trying to forget. I don't care what parts of Europe their forebears came from, or how they got here, or what high crimes and misdemeanors they may have committed along the way."

His shoulders slumped. "Rats," he said. "Here I thought I had this brilliant idea for a present, and it turns out to be the last thing in the world that you'd want."

CHRISTMAS CAME, AND Alden's gift to me was a pair of driving gloves—which, I couldn't help thinking, would keep me from leaving traces of Touch DNA on the steering wheel, a thought I was happy to push aside.

My gift to him, along with the clothes Louella had chosen, was a boxed set of eight books by an English veterinarian, published in the 1970s and popular bestsellers in their day. Alden had come across one of the books in the school library and liked it enough to read some passages aloud at the dinner table, but it hadn't occurred to him to seek out the rest of the man's work.

I tracked them down on line—no daunting task, as like no end of books in the internet age they were hiding in plain sight. He was delighted. "I knew he wrote more books," he said, "but that was the only one in the library. I didn't realize you could just, like, *find* them out there."

But he knew what else you could find, and had gifted his mother and sister accordingly, having swabbed their cheeks earlier for what he told them was a school assignment. It was for biology lab, he explained, and would consist of examining epithelial cells under the microscope.

"Which we actually did," he said, during the opening of the presents. "But I just used my own cells for that, and it was more about getting comfortable using the microscope than what was going to turn up on the slide. But with you guys, well, I didn't want to spoil the surprise."

And I suppose he didn't want to risk having them opt out the way I had.

He'd bought himself a present as well, an ethnic analysis of his own DNA, and now he helped interpret everybody's results. His own makeup came in at 87% British Isles, 6% German and 4% French, with the rest essentially unidentifiable.

Rottweiler, Kristin suggested.

"See, now what this does," he said, "it tells us something about my father. Not about Dad, but Duane Allen Shipley, you know, my biological father. See, when we look at Mom's data we see that *her* DNA's still mostly British Isles, like 74%, with the rest about half and half German and French."

"My mother's mother," Louella said. "There were Pennsylvania Dutch on that side of the family. That would account for the German. I don't know where the French part would come in."

Given the way the France and Germany abutted, and the long history of war and territorial give and take, that much genetic intermingling seemed likely enough. We batted that around some, and agreed that the Shipley contribution would have been exclusively British Isles.

"Which makes me pretty much white bread all the way," Alden said. "Which I more or less figured, but I sort of hoped something interesting would turn up. A great-great-grandfather who was part African or Asian or, I don't know, Arapaho? Or maybe Jewish, but something to make me a little less boring."

Louella told him he was pretty interesting, no matter where his genes came from.

"Now with Sis here," he said, "you can see right away that we're half-siblings."

"And I'm the better half," Kristin pointed out. "And it's not that different. I'm still mostly British Isles, same as you."

He went over her profile with her. Her DNA was predominantly British Isles, but the figure they supplied was 65% for her as opposed to 87% for him. The French component was the same, but German was a little higher, and much of the remainder was identified as Scandinavian, with a 3% dash of Native American in the mix.

The Scandinavian didn't surprise me. I'd almost forgotten, but remembered now, that there were cousins on my mother's side named Olson. Boisterous and athletic, as I recalled, but I'd never really known any of them, or anything about them.

If Kristin was 3% American Indian, my own percentage would presumably be twice that. Which was enough to be real (assuming the analysis was accurate) but what did that amount to? One great-great grandparent? You'd have to go back a few generations to find a Comanche in the woodpile.

AFTERWARD, AWAY FROM the others, Alden apologized. "All I thought," he said, "was it would be interesting to know Kristin's genetics, and it was all in the mail before I got that it'd mean poking into your background, because, you know, half of her DNA comes from you."

Unless, of course, it was someone else who'd fathered her. But that possibility never occurred to either of us. The physical resemblance was unmistakable, and Kristin's mannerisms and facial expressions were an echo of mine, as was her sense of humor. She was my daughter, and half her DNA was mine.

I told him not to worry about it. What was it all anyhow besides a few numbers and countries of origin?

"And it's not like there's anything exotic in the print-out," he said. "And all it is anyway is DNA, you know? I mean, you're still my dad, right? No matter where my DNA came from."

I was touched by that, and assured him he was my son and I was his father, and that our recognizing the fact implied no disloyalty to Duane Shipley. I told him I was proud of him, and he told me he loved me, and it was a very nice moment.

And everything was going to be fine, I told him, even as I told myself.

AND WHY WOULDN'T it be?

Because my individual DNA profile was still nowhere to be found. Kristin's was on file at the firm charged with duly analyzing the swabs Alden had mailed in, but Kristin hadn't left her DNA all over a dead woman in California. A CSI-style computer, flashing its lights to show off for the television audience, wouldn't suddenly flash *Match Match Match* while its screen showed us her picture.

My secret and I were as safe as we'd ever been.

DID I REALLY believe that?

I told myself I did, and perhaps it was so, because in certain respects belief is largely a matter of what you tell yourself. Do you believe in God? Do you believe in life after death? In reincarnation? In life on other planets? If you believe in any of these, isn't it because you've elected to believe?

Oh, evidence may play a part, but it's like evidence in a judicial proceeding, with each side citing it as proof. Perhaps you remember the cartoon, two goldfish in a bowl. "If there's no God, then who changes our water?"

You believe what you want to believe.

MY FAITH IN the matter, let's be clear, was no Rock of Ages, firm and unyielding. I couldn't help knowing that forensic technology was continuing to evolve at the speed of one of those flashing CSI computers, that what they could do yesterday was less than they can do today, and barely a shadow of what they'd be able to accomplish tomorrow.

To keep everything in perspective, you ought to understand that the subject did not occupy my mind every moment of every day. Indeed, I had a life to live, and I spent my time living it. I had a business to run and I ran it. I had my clubs, Lions and Kiwanis and Rotary, and rarely missed a meeting. I bowled on Tuesday nights, and from my chair in front of the TV I followed the Bengals and Buckeyes, the Cincinnati Reds, the Indy Pacers, all in their respective seasons, and without ever really caring how the games turned out.

If there was nothing compelling on television, I might be in my home office, possibly seated in this chair in front of this computer, keeping up with email or walking the unmarked trails of the internet. But more often than not instead of booting up the computer I'd be in my recliner with my feet up, reading one book or another. I'd had a good run with Civil

War history, but something had pointed me toward Rome, and I was having a go at Gibbon.

The Decline and Fall of the Roman Empire. I'm sure an abridged edition would have told me as much as I needed to know, but I'd come upon a set of six boxed volumes online at a very good price, and before I knew it I'd signed on for the long haul. It proved to be absorbing for all that it was slow going, and I was in no hurry to get to the end. I mean, I already knew how it turned out.

And didn't I have all the time in the world?

PERHAPS NOT.

TV fare: *Dateline, 48 Hours, Forensic Files.* Sometimes those shows were what I wanted to watch. Other times they found their way unbidden to our large high-definition screen, and more often than not they drew me in.

When they didn't, the nightly news was obliging enough to come up with the occasional item. A man who'd served twenty years for rape and murder was released when DNA exonerated him—although the prosecutor still swore he was guilty.

And, while the lucky man's enterprising attorneys were suing the state for some optimistic sum, surely no more than a drop in the bucket for all those years the system had stolen from their client, his prison cell didn't stay empty for long.

Cold cases, capital crimes long forgotten by all concerned, were being solved and resolved left and right.

All over America, rape kits and crime scene evidence lay in storage. While everyone had known for years that the cases would never be solved and the evidence would never prove useful, it was apparently easier to kick the evidentiary can down the road than to clear the shelves and make room for the next batch of rape kits.

So it had been for years and years. And now specialists of a new sort, cold case investigators, were going through old files and processing old rape kits.

And making new arrests.

Sometimes scientific advances enabled them at last to build cases against men they'd suspected all along. In other instances, men who'd never raised the slightest blip on the radar screen, men who'd never been linked in any way to the case or the victim, were suddenly caught in the investigators' crosshairs, under arrest and charged with having committed a crime they and the world barely remembered.

But not all of them were there to be found. One *48 Hours* episode brought an earlier show up to date, documenting the solution of a thirty-three-year-old rape and murder in Kearney, Nebraska. The victim was a recent high school graduate, engaged to a classmate who'd been the prime suspect until alibi witnesses cleared him. Now DNA indicated she'd been killed by a man who'd evidently never met her until the day he raped and strangled her. He was a unemployed day laborer, forty-four years old, passing through Kearney on his way home to Grand Island, and how they met and what passed between them we'll never know, because by the time his DNA pointed to him he was as dead as she was, spirited away by liver cancer before the law took the slightest interest in him.

48 Hours couldn't show Kearney cops making an arrest, or even knocking on a door in Grand Island. By the time cancer got him, the perpetrator had moved several times, winding up in Alpine, Texas. The best feature of the updated show was an interview with the officer, now retired, who'd been on the case at the very beginning.

"You have to wonder what good it does after all these years," he told the camera. "I promised Vicki's parents I'd find the person who'd done this, who took her away from them, and I guess I thought I would, but then I came to know I wouldn't. And then the father passed, and once a year I'd call on the mother, just to let her know somebody still cared. And then *she* died, and just two years ago Ken Silbergaard, and that was the worst part for me."

Silbergaard was the victim's fiancé, cleared thirty years ago.

"We knew he didn't do it, but we couldn't say who did, and I know there were people who were never entirely sure about Ken. Maybe he was genuinely innocent and maybe he managed to get away with it, and as long as the case was unsolved there was a shadow falling on him. Who knows how different his life might have been otherwise? I wish he'd lasted long enough for me to apologize to him. I don't know what I did that I could have done any different, but still, you know?"

THAT SENT ME to Google. I'd never even considered the possibility of collateral damage in the death of Cindy Raschmann. Grieving parents? A boyfriend under suspicion?

I couldn't find anything, and I was reluctant to look too hard. Anything I did online would leave evidence, on my computer if nowhere else.

Early on the cyberworld had appeared to be one in which anything could vanish forever with a single keystroke. You hit DELETE and the slate was clean.

Except I'd come to realize the opposite was true, and that anything done on a computer had a half-life that was essentially eternal. You could delete it all you pleased, and a teenager who knew what he was doing could find it somewhere on your hard drive.

If you removed the hard drive and pulverized it, if you consigned the whole computer to a river bottom, that might be enough. But if you backed up your data automatically to another drive, that was one more thing you had to deal with. And if you backed up everything automatically to the Cloud—whatever that is, exactly—well, you were screwed, weren't you?

But why should I worry about records of my Google searches? There's this unending document I'm working on at this very moment, utterly incriminating from its opening sentence onward. "A man walks into a bar." And so he does, and it's all here, where anyone could read it.

It's password-protected, so at least I don't have to worry about one of the kids borrowing Dad's computer for a quick check of Instagram and stumbling onto evidence that the old man is a monster.

If I should come to the attention of the authorities, if the long arm of the law should manage to reach all the way to Lima, the password would prove about as impenetrable as the lock on a motel room door, and at least as easy to kick in. Any geek assigned the task of cracking my computer would manage the trick without breaking a cybersweat.

Really, none of it mattered. If they had reason to look at me, they had me cold.

All the more reason to avoid anything that might supply such a reason. For years I'd done fine leaving well enough alone. I was no longer certain that "well enough" was still an apt description of the Cindy Raschmann case, but if not I was still best advised to keep my hands off it.

Which was easier said than done.

You know how it is when you nick yourself? A slip while shaving, a scrape on the back of one's hand, anything sufficient to break the skin. A little bleeding—enough to spread your DNA around, I suppose—and then it scabs over and that's the end of it.

Except the healing process sometimes includes itching, and one responds automatically, even unconsciously, by scratching. One's fingers want nothing so much as to pick at the scab.

I kept holding myself back from reaching for a telephone, punching in a number.

Oh, I made that phone call over and over in the silent privacy of my own mind. *Hi, this is George Haycock, I'm researching techniques in cold case investigation. I wondered if there'd been any recent development in an old case of yours. This one's all the way back in 1968. The victim's name is—give me a minute here—Raschmann? First initial's C as in Charlie?*

Endless variations. I tried on different identities and different motives for my quest. I was a freelance journalist, following up a piece I'd done on the California Highway Killer. I was a deputy sheriff in Oregon running down a lead in one of my own cases. But every silent rehearsal was essentially the same: I was some voice in the shadows, wanting to be reassured the Cindy Raschmann case was stalled and unlikely to be reopened. No developments, no progress, no reason to open that file and sift old evidence or run down old leads that went nowhere.

That's what I wanted, of course, but to pick up the phone and dial the number was to risk its very opposite. *Some dude asking about Cindy Raschmann, and that reminds me. Shouldn't somebody be taking a new look at that? Maybe a fresh pair of eyes'll see something we missed. With all the advances, all the new crap the scientists keep coming up with . . .*

And I knew this, and reminded myself of it over and over again, and on each occasion squelched the impulse. But God, how the scab itched! I laid a tentative fingertip on it time and time again, and each time I managed to keep myself from picking at it. I would hold off, and the itch would subside.

For the time being.

"I HAD THIS email," Alden said.

A few hours ago I was sitting where I am now, at this desk in what had been his room until we fitted out his aerie in the attic. I had finished the most recent entry, and after reading "*For the time being*" several times over, I'd decided that was as good a place as any to stop. I saved what I'd written, closed the file, and moved on to my own email. There was nothing of great interest, and certainly nothing that had anything to do with DNA or crime scene investigation or a woman who'd died decades ago and two thousand miles away.

But I found something to click on, and it led to something else, and I was miles away myself, learning about the breeding habits of a freshwater aquarium fish named *Copeina arnoldi*, more commonly known as the splash tetra. I don't keep aquarium fish, or have any interest in them. Kristin had kept a small goldfish in a glass bowl (and changed the water, like God in the cartoon), but it had died, and so had its replacement, and she'd since decided that Chester the putative Rottweiler was all the companion animal she needed. The empty goldfish bowl had long since been retired to a basement storage shelf.

So I had no reason to read about the splash tetra, but the internet doesn't ask of you all that much in the way of motivation, and what I learned about the fish was interesting enough to keep me reading. And that's what I was doing when Alden came into the room and said he'd had an email.

I looked up.

"It was actually addressed to Kristin," he said, "but as far as they're concerned we've both got the same email address.

Some people call it an eDress, with a small E and a capital D, because otherwise it looks like you were trying to write *address* and made a typo. But when you say it out loud it sounds dumb."

I might have urged him, gently, to get to the point. But I knew what the point was, and I was in no hurry for him to get there.

"What they do," he said, "and I didn't know this when I sent in the samples, or if I did know it I wasn't thinking of it, you know? Like it slipped my mind, and that's if it was ever there in the first place."

I waited. Why hurry him?

"They take your DNA and compare it to the samples they have on file. It's not like on TV—bing-bing-bing-bing MATCH! MATCH! MATCH!—because there's never a complete match, because your DNA is like, unique."

"Right."

"But they come up with relatives you didn't know you had. Or ones you did, because they found what they said was a very probable first cousin of Kristy's right here in Ohio, and guess who it turned out to be? Me, because I guess they don't have an algorithm for *half-brother*, so in their books I'm her, quote, *very probable first cousin*."

Was that it? It was unsettling all by itself, in its implications and what it boded for the future, but I could tell there was more.

"So actually that was last week. And then they told me about a second or third cousin of mine in downstate Illinois. I mean, down around Cairo, except they pronounce it Kay-ro."

"Shows what they know."

"And people call that part of the state Little Egypt, and from what you hear, everybody down there's an inbred re-tard in the Ku Klux Klan, and they only find out about DNA when they get arrested for incest, if that's even considered a crime down there. I mean, that's the sort of thing you hear. I'm sure it's like an exaggeration."

"I suspect you're right."

"Anyway, some woman knew enough about DNA to send them hers, and her profile matches enough of my markers for us to be cousins. She's not a match for anybody else, so that puts her on the Shipley side of the family."

"Are you going to get in touch with her?"

"Maybe. I don't know. Maybe she'll reach out to get in touch with me, and then I can decide." He grinned. "I had this thought, like I'd write and she'd write and we'd get together, and she'd be hot and gorgeous and there'd be this strong at-traction between us, and there we are and we can't do a thing about it because we're cousins and we both know it."

"A twenty-first century problem," I said.

"I mean it's just me daydreaming, because for all I know she weighs three hundred pounds, with one blue eye and one brown eye and they're only half an inch apart after a couple of centuries of Little Egypt inbreeding. But yeah, a twenty-first century problem is right, because suppose your biological fa-ther was a sperm donor? And nobody who donated sperm just did it once. There was this thing on TV, or maybe it was online, I don't remember which, but all over America clusters of people are finding out they've got the same sperm donor for a daddy, and they never met him but they're walking around full of his DNA."

We talked about that a little, because it was an interesting subject all by itself. For thirty or forty years, a college student could go once or twice a week to a clinic, sit in a room with a copy of *Playboy,* jerk off into a cup, and walk away with a few dollars for his trouble. And that was all there was to it, and why would he ever give it a second thought? If his efforts resulted in a pregnancy, he wouldn't know about it, and neither would anyone ever know of his role in the proceedings.

All changed now.

"So I don't know," he said. "Whether I'll do anything about my retarded third cousin. I think I'll let it go, at least for now."

We agreed it was probably best to put off the decision for the time being. But he wouldn't have interrupted me to report a possible Shipley cousin two states away. There was another shoe, and I waited for it to drop.

"The thing is," he said, "it turns out there's a couple of third or fourth cousins out west."

"Cousins of yours?"

He shook his head.

"Kristin's, then."

A nod. A forty-four-year-old woman in Washington State and man in his early twenties in Salt Lake City.

"So they'd be, you know, relatives of yours. You'd be the connection between them and Kristy." We both let that sentence hang in the air, and then he said, "I'm not saying anything to Kristy."

"No."

"Dad, I'm just so sorry I went ahead and started all of this. I was stupid, I didn't stop to think that swabbing Kristy's cheek was like swabbing yours from a distance."

"With a really long Q-tip," I said.

"Yeah, right. The thing is, I never meant for this to happen. Not that anything's happened, not really, and nothing will, because the only way anyone can try to get in touch with Kristin Lynne Thompson is through my email address, and anything that gets to my mailbox I'll just delete."

As if it could be that simple. As if anything in our age would ever again be truly delible.

WE MUST HAVE scattered, we Bordens. That was our last name, Borden, like Elsie the Cow and her husband Elmer, famous for his glue. Or like Lizzie, as you prefer.

Borden. I let Word perform a Global Search of this document to confirm that I had just now written my original surname for the first time in all the years since I signed over my car's title to a dealer in Fort Wayne.

The ten little Bordens and how they grew. I've had some time to remember the names, and it's interesting what comes back to you if you give it a chance. Judy and Rhea, Arnie and Hank and Roger and Charlotte—*and* Tom and Lucas, Carole and Joyce. With the youngest four, two boys and two girls, I can't remember their birth order, can't attach faces or any other specifics to their names. And I'm not a hundred percent certain of some of those names. Was it Luke or Lucas, Joyce or Joy? Was it just-plain-Carol or Carole-with-an-E?

I may not have known then. I don't think the younger ones were ever all that clear in my mind. I'm afraid I never paid them much attention.

And now, for the first time in a while, I found myself wondering what had become of them. My parents would certainly be long gone by now, and my father surely would have died well-insured. And my brothers and sisters? It seemed a good bet that some of them would be alive, even as one or two of them would probably not.

Judy and Rhea might be grandparents. Even great-grandparents, if their own early training in motherhood had got them off to an early start. Arnie, Hank, Charlotte, Luke, Carole, Joyce, Tom—where had you all gone off to, and how many marriages and divorces could you claim? And how many offspring?

I had never cared enough to pose the question. I still didn't care, not really, but the questions came regardless.

ROGER. THAT WAS my name, Roger Edward Borden. I never liked it. Much better to walk around in a castoff shirt with *Buddy* on the pocket, better to answer to Buddy than to Roger.

Roger Wilco. Roger the Dodger.

I don't suppose there's anything genuinely wrong with the name. It's neither dirt common nor weirdly unusual.

But I'd never liked being Roger.

LAST NIGHT, AFTER the others were asleep, I looked at the gun.

It was in the lowest of the three drawers on the right-hand side of my desk. That was the drawer that you could lock, and so that's where I'd put the thing back when I acquired the desk. Years and years ago, that would have been, and I don't remember where I'd kept it before.

Or when I'd last looked at it, and consequently I had to search the desk's other drawers, the unlocked ones, until I found the key. If nothing else, it put paid to the argument that I kept the gun for protection. Any intruder could kill all of us several times over before I could get my hands on the thing.

But I did in fact find the key, eventually, and I was able to turn the lock, and the gun that time forgot was waiting where I'd left it.

The sight of it in the otherwise empty drawer, the feel of it when I took it in my hand, brought back flashes of memory. One of them reminded me how I'd sniffed the barrel all those years ago, trying to determine if it had been recently fired. The results, I recalled, were inconclusive.

I repeated the action, but this time what I smelled was the

steel of which the gun had been made and the gun oil with which I'd cleaned it before placing it in the drawer. That came back to me, coming across the gun-cleaning kit on a basement shelf at Thompson Dawes, bringing it home, and cleaning the thing in the manner explained in the kit's instruction sheet.

Where was the kit? Wouldn't I have put it in the drawer as well?

I don't believe I've described the instrument itself. It's a five-shot Colt revolver with a two-inch barrel, and there's a .38-Special cartridge in each of its five chambers. This was not the case when it came into my hands. At first it had in fact appeared to be fully loaded, but there were spent cartridges in three of its chambers and live rounds in only two.

And so it had remained until the day I cleaned it. The details had slipped my mind, but sitting there with gun in hand brought them back. When I cleaned the gun with the kit I'd found, I had cleared all five chambers, and the following day I'd disposed of everything, the kit included, in the store's trash.

Thompson Dawes didn't stock guns, which had made the discovery of the kit a surprise, but I'd never paid much attention to the basement, and now I had a look around to see what other wonders it might hold. Porter Dawes had evidently sold firearms at one point, phasing them out before I went to work for him; I didn't find any, but I did uncover some supplies—another cleaning kit, the same as the one I'd used, and two boxes of shotgun shells, and a variety of handgun and rifle bullets.

It all went in the dumpster, but not before I'd transferred

five .38-Special rounds from their box to my jacket pockets, where they weighed more than I would have guessed. I didn't know if they'd fit, but as far as I could tell they were identical to the live rounds I'd discarded, and when I got home that evening I eased the burden on my pockets and filled the Colt's empty chambers.

The bullets seemed to fit well enough. I knew, as must be obvious, next to nothing about guns, and had no way of knowing whether a pull on the trigger would result in a gunshot or a mere *click*. I could have found out readily enough through the simplest of experiments, but why? With the revolver locked forever in its drawer, what difference did it make whether or not it was capable of firing a bullet?

Then why load it in the first place?

A fair question. I'm not sure I raised the question at the time. I doubt I'd have bothered to load the gun, not if I'd had to go out and buy ammunition for it. But those five rounds were in a box of shells I was in the process of discarding, they weren't costing me anything, not even the effort of a trip to a gun store, and if one were going to keep a gun in a locked desk drawer, shouldn't it be a loaded gun? Shouldn't it be ready for use, even if one were never likely to use it?

Never mind. I didn't give it much thought then, if any. No need to overthink it now.

So. Last night I found the key, unlocked the drawer, drew it open. I took the gun in hand, felt its weight, breathed in its smell of steel and gun oil.

I did not hold the gun to my temple, or put the barrel in

my mouth. I did not tighten my finger on the trigger and squeeze off a shot.

I did not do any of those things. But I did imagine myself doing them.

For what it's worth.

THAT THIRTY-THREE-YEAR-OLD case in a city in Nebraska I can't be bothered to look up. It'll come to me.

The killer, the man who got away with it for all those years, who went to his grave without ever being suspected of anything, had left his semen in the girl he'd raped and strangled. And years later the cold case investigators worked up his DNA profile and checked it against the state and federal databases.

And came up empty, because the man they were looking for wasn't there to be found. Aside from a handful of traffic violations and a couple of DUI arrests, one of which got his driver's license suspended for six months, he'd gone through the rest of his life without making a mark on a police blotter. I can't say that his was an exemplary life, and for all I know he'd killed again, but if he'd done so he'd left no evidence behind.

So they ran the DNA he'd left in Kearney—that was the city, I knew it would come to me, and he wasn't from Kearney, he was from some nearby town, and it'll come to me, too. And indeed it has. Grand Island. He killed her in Kearney, he went home to Grand Island.

But that's not the point. The point is that they ran his DNA and came up empty, and that was the end of that, except of course it wasn't. Another year and another technical development, and while the possibility that he might be a direct descendant of Charlemagne hadn't prompted him to swab his cheek and mail if off to Ancestors R Us, some relatives were not so discreet.

And, just as a fortyish woman in Washington State and a younger man in Utah had pinged when my daughter's DNA showed up, so did the Kearney Killer's relatives light up the screen when someone took a good look.

On some of the cold case shows they tell you how, after a fresh look at forensic evidence points to a suspect, the cops have to shadow him for weeks waiting for him to spit on the sidewalk or discard a paper cup, thus giving them lawful access to his DNA. In this case, there was nobody around to cast a shadow. A court order allowed them to exhume a grave in West Texas, and they didn't need the consent of the deceased to take a sample of his DNA.

Bingo! A perfect match.

Case closed.

MAYBE SOMEONE IN Bakersfield, or more likely somebody with California's state equivalent of the FBI, had already begun submitting the DNA from Cindy Raschmann to the various who's-your-daddy sites. Maybe the outfit Alden had selected had already received California's query, and maybe the results had already popped up on their screen.

Any or all of these things might already have happened. And if they hadn't, they would. And someone in California would put in a request, and someone in Sacramento would approve a trip to Ohio, and the next thing you knew there'd be two men on our front porch, ringing our doorbell.

They show up in pairs, don't they? But it wouldn't necessarily be two men, not nowadays. It could be a man and a woman. It could even be two women, theoretically, but that seemed less likely.

They could be out there right now, while I sit here imagining them. They could be driving past the house, figuring out their approach. The process, in fact, could be anywhere at all along the timeline, and the question of how far they'd come showed itself as immaterial.

Because it was all just a matter of time, and the amount of time didn't matter. They were coming. And I wasn't going anywhere.

THAT LAST ENTRY was three days ago. The day before yesterday I booted up the computer and read the last thing I'd written. I closed the file and went on gazing at the blank screen.

Shut it down, went to the kitchen, got a beer out of the refrigerator. Looked at it, put it back, chose a ginger ale instead. Sat on the porch with it, watched the passing traffic. There's not much of it, not on our little street, but cars do pass by now and then.

I found myself noticing the license plates, realized I was looking for an out-of-state tag. But they wouldn't have driven here from California. They'd have flown and rented a car. Or some cooperative local officer would be driving them around.

The ginger ale was sweet. Artificially sweetened, in fact. It's a brand Louella likes. I don't know that she has to worry about calories, but she would rather enjoy the sweetness without taking in the sugar.

"Although it seems like cheating," she said once.

What am I going to do about her? About all of them?

YESTERDAY, A DAY after the ginger ale on the porch, was the day for my usual visit to Penderville. I called my manager, invented a reason to cancel our lunch, said I'd try to get down there sometime in mid-afternoon.

"But just in case," I said, and we had as much of a conversation as we needed to have.

Around four I got on I-75, headed for Penderville. I stayed on past the exit I usually took, and pulled into the parking lot for a restaurant called Crazy Jane's. The red neon sign, which had caught my eye over the years, showed a woman in profile. Jane, I suppose, though there was nothing obviously crazy about her.

I parked, and after a few minutes I got out of the car.
A man walks into a bar.

THERE WERE PERHAPS a dozen customers, all of them from age groups a good deal younger than my own. A man and a woman in a booth, three men at a table, the rest perched on barstools. A head or two turned to note my entrance, then turned away.

A country song played, a woman singing. I couldn't make out the words.

The bartender was a woman, her cap of hair so blond it was white. At first glance I'd taken her for a man because she had that haircut they give you at Marine boot camp. But her face was feminine enough, if a little hard, and the short shorts and halter top displayed a woman's body, and an attractive one in the bargain.

I ordered a beer, and she said they had PBR on tap. Was that all right?

I nodded, and she'd drawn the beer before I'd managed to decipher the initials. Pabst Blue Ribbon, of course.

"Sit anywhere," she said.

I carried the glass to a table along the wall and thought about her haircut, wondering whether it was a nod to fashion or a personal statement in some area of sexual politics.

I imagined myself asking her, my hands on her throat

making it impossible for her to reply. She would be strong, but this was my fantasy, so I would be stronger.

A thought came unbidden. Maybe it wasn't a haircut, maybe she'd lost all her hair to a round of chemotherapy.

Maybe she'd already survived a greater peril than I could pose, even in the privacy of my mind.

A record ended, another began to play. A male vocalist this time, but the lyrics were no easier to make out.

I took a sip, finally, of my PBR. When she'd said the initials, the very first thought that came to me was Peanut Butter and Jelly. I'd recognized that as wrong, and the next thing I thought of was NPR, for National Public Radio, and then Pabst came finally to mind, a rather distant third.

It tasted fine.

I generally keep Heineken in the refrigerator, and a six-pack lasts a long time. It was a Heineken I'd picked up and put back the other day in favor of a diet ginger ale.

I picked up the glass to take another sip, put it down without doing so. I thought, *The beer that made Milwaukee famous.* Wasn't that a song? A slogan first, of course, but then there was the song, how the beer that made Milwaukee famous made a fool out of me. Or a jackass, or some other two-syllable word.

Except that was Schlitz, wasn't it? That claimed to have made Milwaukee famous?

A loser, that was the word. *What made Milwaukee famous made a loser out of me.*

Jesus, what fucking difference did it make?

HOW LONG WAS I there? Half an hour?

Long enough for a few more songs to play, long enough for one of the loners at the bar to depart, long enough for two others to replace him. Long enough for me to abandon the fantasy I'd been attempting to build around Maggie.

That was the bartender's name. I heard a customer call her by name, which made her a little less anonymous, and a little less suitable for the use I was trying to make of her. I found myself recalling things about her I'd barely noted during our brief transaction. A small tattoo on her wrist, apparently a cryptic Chinese symbol. A larger one on her shoulder, which I took at first to be a crayfish—and then forgot about, and then remembered and decided was more likely to be a scorpion.

Which might mean she was a Scorpio, born in the autumn. Or that she had or used to have a Scorpio lover. Or that the creature was her totem animal, chosen as such for reasons at which I could only guess.

I knew nothing about her, but knowing this much made her a little bit more of a person, and turned what I was attempting to do in the privacy of my imagination into an offense against her person. That she was unaware of it, that I was to her no more than an old man with a beer sitting almost invisible in the shadows, that she'd very likely forgotten me altogether—none of this seemed to mitigate my crime.

There was another woman, the one in the booth. I couldn't really make out what she looked like, so I let my imagination flesh her out as it preferred. And in my mind I sent her companion to the restroom, and lured her out of the place before he returned, and—

Never mind.

I guess I was inside Crazy Jane's for half an hour, maybe forty-five minutes at the outside. My glass of PBR was still mostly full when I walked away from it.

My imaginings, redirected from Maggie to the woman in the booth, wouldn't play the game. My mind couldn't stay focused on them. It insisted on wandering, and I gave up and let it wander, and after I'd asked myself for the fourth or fifth time what the hell I was doing there, I did some wandering of my own—out the door and across the parking lot and back behind the wheel of my car.

And I ask myself now what I was doing, and answers bubble up, or seem to.

There was a thought that had come to me as I parked my car. *A sheep as a lamb,* I thought. Shorthand for *You might as well hang for a sheep as a lamb,* that is to say, meaning if I was doomed to be arrested for what I'd done all those years ago, then I might as well update my résumé by doing the same thing once again.

But those five words were the extent of that thought. I'd always known I wasn't going to find a victim in Crazy Jane's. I wasn't looking for one.

And what was I looking for? Really?

I wasn't looking for Cindy Raschmann. Nor was I looking for the MILF who got away.

Maybe I was looking for Buddy.

Looking for the man I'd been, looking to find him lurking within my present self. Because he has to be there, somewhere.

I'm tired. I'm going to bed.

I WONDER WHAT'S going on in Alden's mind.

He must know something.

This evening we had the network news on during dinner, and there was something about a preliminary judicial decision. Could a company voluntarily share its genetic data base with cold case investigators? Could it be compelled to do so? Was the right of privacy of some unwitting relative of a killer thus infringed, and did that right trump the moral imperative to get a dangerous criminal off the streets?

The questions raised seemed to be both legally and morally complicated, and it was evident they would not be resolved overnight. The arguments were familiar, as one heard them often enough in slightly different contexts—when some government agency wanted access to someone's iPhone after a terrorist incident, for example, and Apple refused a court order to unlock it.

At one point I glanced at Alden and caught him looking at me. Our eyes met for only an instant, and I'm not sure I could read anything in his, but I sensed something. Some concern, some perception that the question under examination applied to me in some specific way.

Or maybe I had a spot on my shirt. Maybe there was nothing to be read in his expression, and it was my own ever-present anxiety that made me think otherwise.

The newscast ended with the usual feel-good segment, this one about a woman with two artificial legs who'd just donated a kidney to someone. Louella turned it off, and I suppose we could have talked about that, but instead we picked up on the DNA question.

"It's an argument that keeps coming up in one form or another," I said. "On the one hand you've got the individual's right to privacy, and on the other there's the public's right to security. Changes in technology keep raising new questions. If you commit a crime, or at least give them reason to think you did, they can take you into custody—and take your fingerprints while they're at it, and do a computer check to see if you left those fingerprints at a crime scene in Salt Lake City."

"What crime could somebody commit in Salt Lake City?" Louella wondered. "Monogamy?"

"And they'd arrest you years later," Alden said, "on suspicion of serial monogamy. But I think I see where you're going, Dad. They fingerprint everybody they arrest, and nobody questions their right to do it, because that's been the procedure for years. When did they first start taking people's fingerprints, does anybody know?"

Nobody did. I said they'd been doing it for longer than I could remember, and if anybody ever tried to argue it was an invasion of privacy, nobody'd paid any attention to him.

"DNA's different," I said. "It may vary from state to state, but generally speaking you need a warrant or a court order to obtain a sample."

"Because you're taking something from a person?"

"And invading his person to do it," I said, "although the difference between inking a man's fingertips and swabbing his cheek doesn't seem all that significant, does it?"

"But if he drinks from a cup," he said, "it's not an invasion. That's if it's a paper cup and he throws it away, because if it's in the trash it's fair game. But if he hangs on to the cup and you grab it away from him, then they can throw out the evidence on grounds of whatever it is, unlawful search and seizure?"

"Or not," I said, "depending on what you did and what state you did it in, and what the judge had for breakfast that morning."

"Aren't you glad you're going to be a vet?" Louella asked him. "And not a lawyer?"

"But look what you do every day," Kristin said, shaking a finger at her brother. "Invading the privacy of individuals who can't even argue in their own defense."

We all looked at her.

"When did Chester give you permission to check out his DNA? Maybe he wanted to keep his Rottweiler ancestry private. Did you ever think of that?"

I suspect she was half-serious, as she's got her own way of looking at the world, and a propensity for speaking true words in jest. This time she succeeded in redirecting the conversation, and we were soon engaged, not for the first time, in pointing out to one another the several qualities that elevated our Chester to the pinnacle of dogdom.

I welcomed the change of subject, and had the feeling I wasn't alone in so doing.

Hours later. Alden went to his attic retreat, presumably to do homework. The rest of us watched Jeopardy, *and after the Final Jeopardy entry stumped the six of us—we three Thompsons and all three contestants as well—I came up here and wrote the preceding section.*

And then there was a knock. I turned. Louella, in a nightgown. One I'd given her.

"I'm just so tired," she said, and yawned. "I know it's early, but all of a sudden I can't keep my eyes open."

"Why don't I tuck you in?"

"I don't like to disturb you," she said. "When you're hard at work. But if you're sure you don't mind—"

IT WENT WELL.

And why should that come as a surprise? Ever since I first suggested she feign sleep, that had been unfailingly the way we made love. More often than not it was at her suggestion ("Oh, I can't stop yawning. I'm just so sleepy all of a sudden.")

but some of the time it was I who got the ball rolling ("Honey, I can see how tired you are. Why don't you just close your eyes and let yourself drift off?").

We left my study and went to our bedroom, where she arranged herself on the bed. I was concerned that my visit to Crazy Jane's might get in the way, or that the ghost of Cindy Raschmann would be in the room with us.

But none of this happened. My mind didn't summon up a fantasy starring Maggie the bartender or the woman in the booth or anyone at all, real or imaginary. Some years back I'd let go of the habit of rousing myself with fantasies, invented or remembered, probably because they'd lost their efficacy. It had thus become my habit simply to devote myself to the task of giving pleasure to my partner.

To my wife, that is to say.

To my wife, Louella.

We are older now, and what I feel in my heart and mind does not always empower my loins. But that doesn't seem to matter. Our coupling, whatever form it takes, gratifies us both.

Tonight, surprisingly, I was able to perform in the conventional fashion, and—

No, that's enough. I won't erase what I've just written, but I think it's past time to shut the bedchamber door. And skip a double space, and start afresh.

THERE.

I've just locked the desk drawer, after having unlocked it a few minutes ago. I took the gun in my hand, felt its weight, let my finger rest upon its trigger. I did not point it anywhere, except perhaps in my imagination.

And now it's once more locked away, and the key to the drawer back where I keep it.

There was a gag gift someone gave my father. He kept it on his desk, for a while at least, and I can recall his demonstrating how it worked. It was a little box with a button, and he pressed the button, and the lid lifted, whereupon a disembodied hand emerged from the box with its finger extended. The finger pressed the button, which reversed the entire process, and the hand returned to the box and the lid closed.

I've made a dog's breakfast of describing the process, but perhaps you get the idea. I forget what they called the thing, but it had the word "executive" in the title, and the idea was that you turned it on and its sole function was to turn itself off.

I think I just went through something similar with the gun. I unlocked the drawer in order to lock it again.

IF YOU HAVE a gun on the wall in the first act of your play, you owe it to your audience to see that it's fired before the final curtain.

I don't know who said that. I don't think there were guns

in Shakespeare's plays, I think it was all swords and daggers and poison. So it wouldn't be Shakespeare, and Mark Twain didn't write plays, and neither did Benjamin Franklin.

You could look it up.

Never mind. I've looked it up for you. Anton Chekhov.

WILL I FIRE this gun?

I'd say I've earned the right. It's been hanging on the meta-phorical wall since it came into my possession, and I've men-tioned it often enough in this document that no reader can legitimately claim to be inadequately prepared for whatever role it might play.

If they're going to track me down, if the DNA I left in and on Cindy Raschmann hooks up with some unknown niece or nephew, I'd rather not be around to watch it all play out. My imagination conjures up no end of third-act scenarios, and every last one of them is awful.

Better to get out before it happens.

Do I want to die? No, I honestly don't. I like my life, I like being the man I've become. I love my wife, my son, my daughter.

And there's the rub—and I don't have to look up that line, even I know it's Shakespeare's. Hamlet speaking, to be or not to be.

But there it is. The rub.

I love my wife. I love my son. I love my daughter.

Let me just blurt this out. I never expected to love anybody. I never regarded it as an option. And when I look back at my earlier self, the young lout in the *Buddy* shirt, I see a man who fits every standard definition of a sociopath.

A man with no conscience. A man with no empathy. A man who neither knows nor cares what other people are feeling.

A man who knows right from wrong, even as he knows that the earth is ninety-three million miles from the sun. *Yes, okay, that's nice, I get it, but so what?*

I cannot claim to have made a study of sociopathy, but I've had enough of a personal interest in it to learn something about it. And one conclusion I've drawn, one that seems irrefutable and inescapable, is that there's no cure for the condition. No amount of awareness—of oneself, of the world one lives in—

No, let's make this personal:

No amount of awareness, of myself or of the world I live in, can alter who I am. I may be capable of changing my behavior, even as I crossed a state line, even as I sold one car and bought another, even as I changed my name.

I, who had been a drifter, had evolved into a homeowner. A husband and father, a family man, a creature of settled habits. I'd been in the same line of work almost as long as I'd been in Lima, and I owned the business now, and had enlarged it and made a modest success of it.

I, who had found it within myself to strangle a young woman and violate her dead body, now sat down to dinner every evening with my wife and son and daughter. And bowled in a league once a week. And—

Enough.

What, then, had become of Buddy? Had he been some sort of sociopathic larval stage, and had he subsequently emerged from his chrysalis a fully evolved human being?

It would be nice to think so.

But I sit here, staring at my computer screen, staring beyond it at the person I am and the life I've led, and it's just not so, is it?

Buddy hasn't gone anywhere. He's still here. He acts differently, and in certain respects he sees himself and the world differently.

But has he grown a conscience?

No, I was quick to type just now, but then I backed up to amend it. Let's make it *Yes and no.*

Because I am aware, in a way and to an extent that Buddy never was, of what I ought to do. And I have become in the habit over the years of following the suggestions of that particular inner voice.

Because it's right? Because it's what God or some equivalent thereof, some Divine stand-in, wants me to do? Because I'll feel better about myself if I do the right thing?

No, I don't think so.

I think I've learned that it's prudent for me to do what this quasi-conscience prompts me to do. It's in my interest, and I'm able to act in my own interest and override contrary impulses. In fact I've done so for long enough that I'm barely aware of those impulses.

But I continue, in my heart of hearts, in my essential self, to be a sociopath.

Let me be candid, even though my fingers balk at typing the words. I am sitting here, weighing possible courses of action circumstances might lead me to take. I have just told you that I love my wife, my son, my daughter.

And one course of action I find myself weighing, and indeed considering quite dispassionately, would have me annihilating my family.

Killing them all. Killing Louella, killing Alden, killing Kristin.

IT'S BEEN THREE days since the last entry. After I typed their names I sat looking at the screen, reading that paragraph over and over. I tried to find something else to write, to add to what I'd written, and what words came to me didn't seem worth recording.

After a while I shut down the computer and went to bed.

And fell asleep right away, and slept soundly. And got up in the morning and took up my life where I'd left it, and didn't walk into this home office of mine until evening, after the news and after *Jeopardy*. Opened the file, read the last three paragraphs, sat there thinking or not thinking for perhaps five minutes, and then shut things down again.

Did the same thing the following day. The day after that—which I guess was yesterday—I didn't even come in here.

Stood at the door, couldn't think what I'd write, couldn't think why I'd want to write anything.

I thought of the gun. Thought about Chekhov. Went downstairs to see what was on TV.

And here I am now.

IT WOULD BE to spare them.

And that makes its particular sense to me, even as I recognize the notion as utterly ridiculous. Here are three people, three for whom I care as I never thought myself capable of caring for anyone, three people leading lives they clearly enjoy—and I actually find myself entertaining the thought of ending those lives.

I'm sure you find the thought appalling. I assure you that it is no less appalling to the man whose thought it is.

But if I don't?

Because, you see, even as I love them, so do they love me. I'm the loving husband of one, the loving father of the others. While I rather doubt that they confuse me with Christ or Confucius or Captain America, and while I trust that there is something clear-eyed and balanced in their love, they surely think far more highly of me than I could ever think of myself.

They think I'm a good man.

And why shouldn't they? I've never given them cause to think otherwise. In the life I've led, the life of which they've been a part, I have acted the part of a good man.

I've given a good performance. I've even managed at times to convince myself.

But what happens when the police cars pull up in front of our house? What happens when our doorbell rings and one of us answers it?

What happens when it all goes pear-shaped?

Disbelief, for a starter. They've made a mistake, they've come to the wrong house, they've got the wrong man. Somehow or other an error has been made, and somehow or other the husband and father they know and cherish has been linked to an atrocious act which could only have been committed by someone else.

But belief would come, quickly or slowly. One way or another, they would know the truth.

And then? I don't know what would happen after that. I can envision any number of futures, but can't know which one lies in store for us. Because we have free will? Or only because the predetermined scripts of our lives have been withheld from us?

Subjectively it would seem to amount to the same thing. The one thing that's clear to me about the future is that it is to be dreaded. They will know the truth about me, as will everyone with whom I'm acquainted, all my fellow Kiwanians and Rotarians and Lions, the fellows I bowl with, the workers I employ . . .

And so on. The customers at the stores, in Lima and in Penderville. Everyone living in the area, really, everyone who looks at a television set or picks up a newspaper.

People I don't know. People I've never met and will never

meet. People all over the world, people who but for the miracle of DNA would never have heard of John James Thompson or Roger Borden or, God help us, Cindy Raschmann.

Of course I don't have to hang around and see it through. I don't need to find a lawyer and watch it all play out. Right now, sitting here, I could unlock the lower right desk drawer and put a bullet in my brain.

And that would end it. Barring the awful irony of life after death, I'd be out of it. It would be over for me.

But for them?

All the rest of the wretched scenario would continue to play out in my absence. Reporters would thrust microphones in Louella's face, seeking details of her life with a rapist and murderer. Alden and Kristin would undergo something similar, and arguably worse.

I'd have gotten off easy, I'd have taken the coward's way out, and I'd have left them to go through no end of hell on their own.

So. Three people, my wife and my son and my daughter, and they were the only persons on earth for or about whom I genuinely cared. If I killed them one by one in their sleep, if each was dead and gone in an instant, then when I went on to take my own life it would be over.

We'd all be safely gone. No one could touch us. No revelation of the truth could shatter our world of illusion, because we'd no longer be in that world or any other.

It would, of course, be a much bigger story than the simple resolution of a long-forgotten cold case. The monster who'd raped and murdered so many years ago would be entirely

subsumed into the far more horrible monster who'd annihi-
lated his entire family.

A bigger story, a more enduring story. But wouldn't it be
that tree falling in the forest, falling soundlessly because there
was no ear present to hear it? If all four of us were gone, what
could it matter what went on in the world we no longer oc-
cupied?

The gun's in the drawer. The drawer is locked. The key is
within my reach.

And here I sit.

Would I be committing the foulest and most despicable
act imaginable, infinitely worse than what I'd done to Cindy
Raschmann?

Or would it be an act of mercy?

I'll have to think about this.

AND DID I?

My routine kept me busy. Up, shower, shave. Breakfast,
and a second cup of coffee with Louella once the kids were
on their way to school.

It was a pleasant morning. I'd have walked to work, but
that would mean walking home at noon, because I'd need the
car to get to my lunchtime Rotary meeting. I'd missed the last
two or three meetings, and I didn't care to lose contact.

The clubs had long since ceased to be important for the
business connections they fostered. Thompson Dawes did

what it did, never failing to turn a profit, never threatening to deliver genuine wealth. We'd survived Walmart and Costco and Home Depot, although each in turn had posed a threat. There'd be no new stores, and no Herculean efforts to grow the business.

A story I heard someone tell. A Scotsman, as thrifty by nature as his countrymen always are in such stories, is in a store inspecting an overcoat. He's concerned about the garment's durability; how long, he asks the saleswoman, is it likely to last?

She looks at him, she looks at the coat, she looks at him, she looks at the coat.

"It'll see ye oot," she says.

And Thompson Dawes will see us oot, yielding a satisfactory income for as long as Louella and I are around to spend it. That's as long as it needs to last. Alden's set on becoming a veterinarian, he's never wavered in his enthusiasm, and it's too early to guess what career might beckon to Kristin, although I can sometimes picture her as a stand-up comedian, or backstage writing lines for someone else to deliver.

Neither of them will want to be selling hammers and nails and pots and pans to the good people of Lima—or Penderville, for that matter. Thompson Dawes might stay in business with a new owner or two—and with a name change, no doubt.

Or the stores could close. I wasn't concerned with leaving a commercial legacy. Neither my name nor that of Porter Dawes needed a spot in Lima's pantheon of retailers.

Things I found myself thinking about, when I wasn't thinking about murder and suicide.

I WENT TO my meeting, heard a story or two, retold the one about the Scotsman and the coat when someone else wondered whether to trade his second car or try to get another year out of it.

"Well, I hope it won't see me oot," he said, "but I guess it'll see me through another model year."

I got caught up on some news, and learned that a man named Charles Kittredge had taken a turn for the worse, and his family had opted for at-home hospice care. I'd known Charles for a good deal longer than I'd been familiar with the word *hospice,* he'd already been an active Rotarian when I came to my first meeting, and while the end had been inevitable for the better part of a year, I hadn't expected it to be this soon.

Charles and I—and it was always Charles, never Charlie or Chuck—were never close, but we saw each other often enough, and always in pleasant circumstances, to make each of us a part of the other's social landscape.

Would I miss him?

I'd go to his funeral. I had the option of seeing him before then, I could contrive to stop by his home for a visit, but I knew I wasn't going to do that. We weren't close enough to warrant it. I'd wait for his death, and send flowers and a note to his widow.

And put on a suit and tie and go to his funeral. And think of him infrequently after that. If at all.

THINGS TO OCCUPY my mind, while I wasn't busy weighing about the pros and cons of killing my family and myself.

"DAD? HAVE YOU got a minute?"

I had written that last paragraph, and spent perhaps five minutes sitting at my desk and looking at it. I couldn't think of anything I wanted to add.

Or to subtract, come to think of it.

And so I shut down and came downstairs and sat in my chair and picked up a novel Louella had read and recommended. So far I hadn't made much headway, and I certainly didn't mind the interruption.

Louella was in the kitchen, Kristin in front of the TV. Alden and I went out on the porch. He started to say something, then broke it off when someone roared by on a motorcycle. When the sound died down he said he wondered what it was like to ride one of those. I said I'd often wondered myself.

"But not enough to find out," I said.

"I'd feel funny," he said. "Making all that noise, interrupting all those conversations."

"I suppose a person gets used to it."

"I suppose. Dad? There was another email. For Kristin, but it came to me."

"Another match."

He nodded. "A man in Scottsdale, Arizona, and he's a closer match than the others. Like he could be an aunt or an uncle. Except he couldn't be an aunt because—"

"Because he's a man."

"Uh, right."

"I don't suppose they gave you his name."

"Actually they did."

"Oh?"

"It's Henry Elmont Borden."

My brother Hank. Had I ever known his middle name? I suppose I must have, but it didn't ring any bells. *Elmont.* A family name, I suppose, and it imparted a certain distinction. There were probably hundreds of Henry Bordens, but there would have to be far fewer with Elmont for a middle name.

"And this email came in today?"

"Actually it was yesterday. I was going to mention it last night, but—"

"But there was no hurry."

"I guess. Was that okay?"

"Perfectly okay," I said. "You want to go for a ride?"

THE RADIO CAME on when I started the engine, tuned to an oldies station. I turned it off and drove with no real destination in mind, letting the car find its way around the outer suburbs.

We were silent a while. Then I said, "Scottsdale's outside of Phoenix. An upscale area, I believe. There's an independent retailers' trade association, Porter Dawes was a longtime member, and the annual dues are low enough that I've never canceled. They've had conventions in Scottsdale. I've never gone, never really considered it, but that's what comes to mind when I think of Scottsdale."

"And this man—"

"Lives there, evidently."

He waited.

"My brother," I said. "Henry, but most people called him Hank. Maybe he goes by Henry now, maybe he calls himself H. Elmont Borden. Was that the middle name? Elmont?"

"That's what it said."

"Henry Elmont Borden. There were ten of us, I had all of these brothers and sisters. I wonder how many of them are still around. I suppose we'll find out, through the miracle of genetic analysis."

"Dad, I never meant for this to happen."

"Don't blame yourself. There was no way for you to see it coming."

"I just didn't think."

And what did he think now? That there was something in the past that I felt a need to avoid, but did he have an idea what it might be?

I looked for a place to pull over, found a strip mall, its handful of stores closed for the day. There were only two vehicles in the lot, a panel truck and an SUV, parked side by side in front of an auto parts outlet. I pulled into a spot at the far end, cut the engine.

"When I first came here," I said, "I had to cross a lot of state lines. I grew up out West."

"I think I knew that."

"What else do you know?"

"Huh?"

"Or suspect. You must have some sense of the situation."

He had his hands in his lap, resting on his seatbelt strap, and his eyes were fastened on them. He said, "I know there's something in the past that could be a problem if it comes to light."

"And can you guess what it might be?"

"Not really." He turned, looked at me. "It really doesn't matter what it is, you know? What you did, or what somebody thought you did, or whatever it was. It's been buried for all these years and all it has to do is stay buried, and if I hadn't been stupid enough to mail off that DNA swab—"

"Then we would have gotten to the same place by some other route," I said. "So you can quit blaming yourself."

"If you say so, but—"

"I was a very different man," I said. "Rootless, drifting. No sense of a social order, no sense of my place in it. No perspective on the thoughts that came to me. Or what I did about them, because I didn't have much in the way of impulse control."

He was sitting in silence, eyes lowered.

"Do you know what a sociopath is?"

"Sort of."

"The definition varies, depending on what dictionary you consult. But if you checked an illustrated dictionary it would show you a picture of Buddy."

"Buddy? Was that what people called you?"

"Only if they were reading the embroidery on my shirt pocket. One of the jobs I had, I was a few years older than you are now. I was pumping gas down in Southern California."

"You weren't still living at home."

I shook my head. "I would pick up a job, sleep in my car until I found a room, hang around for a while, then move on. Pumping gas—this was before gas stations figured out that people could fill their own gas tanks and wipe their own windshields, so they'd pay minimum wage to a guy like me. Someone who had the job before me left this shirt behind, *Buddy* in script on the breast pocket, and it was my size so I got it washed and wore it." I frowned. "I think I got it washed," I said, "but maybe not. I tended to be a little casual about such matters."

He sat there, taking it all in.

"One job I had, I cleaned out the cash register before I took off. But that was because I didn't like the manager's attitude. It's funny, I can picture the man's face, but I can't remember what he did or said or why it bothered me."

"It was a long time ago."

"A very long time ago, and you could say that I was a different person then. And maybe I was and maybe I wasn't."

He didn't say anything, and we let that last sentence hang in the air for a moment.

I said, "I should get to the point. Your mother's probably ready to put dinner on the table. One night after work I was still wearing the Buddy shirt and I went to a bar to get a beer, and I did something. And I'm having trouble coming right out and saying what it was that I did."

"You don't have to say anything, Dad."

"I killed someone," I said.

Another sentence to leave hanging in the air, except this time the words darted around, bounced off the dashboard, echoed and somehow grew louder in the silence. I lowered a window, not so much to let a little air in as to give the words a way out.

"A woman," I said. "Her name was Cindy Raschmann, but I didn't know her name until later, and she never knew mine. All she knew was what it said on my shirt. 'Hey, it's Buddy.' I remember she spoke those words early on. I don't remember anything else she said."

Except for what she'd said so many years later, in what must have been a dream but seemed much more real than any dream I ever had. She'd said those same words again, *Hey, it's Buddy,* and she'd added a few more sentences. I wrote them down earlier when they were fresh in my mind but I won't bother looking for them now.

And then she said *I forgive you.*

"I killed her," I said.

"It was an accident."

What a fine son he was. What a decent and loyal and gen-
erous young man. Could I accept the gift he was offering?

Evidently not.

"It wasn't an accident," I said. "And I wasn't drunk. I'd had
one glass of beer and I don't even think I finished it. We left
the bar together."

Memories flooded in, but I didn't feel the need to find
words for them. I skipped ahead.

"I wound up with my hands around her throat," I said. "I
didn't let go until she was dead."

"AND THEN I *fucked her corpse.*"

But no, I didn't say that.

THE NEXT THING I did say, breaking an extended silence,
was an apology. Not for the act but for the recounting of it.

"I never expected to tell you all this," I said. "I never
thought I'd have reason to. I assumed the past would stay in
the past."

"But I had to go and—"

I stopped him right there. "If you need to blame someone," I said, "stick with Crick and Watson. Once the science
was there, the technology was sure to follow. Then all they

had to do was find uses for it, and everything just kept evolving. *Keeps* evolving, because there's something new every time you turn around. Touch DNA, for God's sake. Early on they needed bodily fluids to get enough cells for a DNA profile. Now any contact between two people transfers enough DNA for them to work with."

"I don't really get how that works," he said, "but I guess it does."

"Say our hands touch," I said, "and some of what's on my hand winds up on your hand. That case a week or two ago on *48 Hours,* the serial rapist who followed women home from Walmart."

"I think it was Target. Like it makes a difference."

"It evidently made a difference to him. I guess you meet a more appealing class of women at Target. He used condoms."

"I remember."

"And disposed of them elsewhere. He wasn't afraid of picking up an STD."

"Or getting anybody pregnant."

"He knew about semen and DNA," I said, "and he thought he was playing it safe. What would he have done if he'd known about Touch DNA? Worn gloves?"

"Or one of those HazMat suits."

I was picturing that, or trying to, and he said, "Dad? After you . . ."

"Killed her," I supplied.

I thought he might flinch at the words, but no. "Then what happened? You just left?"

"Drove for awhile, found a motel room. I was a drifter, so I drifted. It seems to me I was waiting for them to catch me. But they didn't, and I don't know how close they may have come or how much they learned from the crime scene or in the course of their investigation. But then Sirhan Sirhan came along."

"Who?"

"The guy who assassinated Bobby Kennedy."

"Right," he said. "I knew the name, but not how I knew it, and you want to know the first thing I thought just now? That it was the name of a band."

"Or a rapper."

"Li'l Sirhan. This was really a long time ago, wasn't it?" He drew a breath and straightened up in his seat. I picked up the cue, if that's what it was, and keyed the ignition and drove us home.

SOMEWHERE BETWEEN THE strip mall and our house he found an oblique way to ask me if there were any other entries keeping Cindy Raschmann company in my résumé.

I assured him I'd never before done anything of the sort. But I said I had thought about it. It was a fantasy, I said, a longstanding one, and I'd figured that was all it would ever be.

"And you never—"

"Did anything like that again? No, never."

He nodded, grateful for the assurance, but something kept me from leaving it at that. "I thought about it," I said.

"Oh."

"There were times when I might have acted."

"But you didn't."

"No, never. And the impulse—"

"Went away?"

"Subsided," I said.

AT THE DINNER table, it was as if we'd never had the conversation. Louella had made a lamb stew, tweaking a recipe she'd prepared in the past, pepping it up with cumin and cayenne.

"And I used the slow cooker," she said, "instead of the pressure pot. And I must say I felt the slightest bit disloyal."

They looked at her.

"The first conversation I ever had with your father," she said, "was at the store, over a pressure cooker."

"We talked about rhubarb," I said.

"And I brought that pressure cooker home with me, and it's held up perfectly well over the years."

"Better than I have," I said.

"You've both held up beautifully," she said, "and I've never cooked rhubarb in anything else."

How I Met Your Father. Louella reminisced, and I contributed a recollection or two of my own. This wasn't the first trip the four of us had taken down Memory Lane, and Alden and

Kristin seemed as usual to enjoy this back-in-the-day glimpse of their parents.

I had to wonder, though, what Alden made of it, now that our conversation at the strip mall had put me in a different light. Or could he just wall that off and keep it at a safe distance from the rhubarb and the pressure cooker?

WHEN WE LEFT the table I told Alden I'd be upstairs in my office. "Why don't you give me, oh, half an hour? Forty-five minutes?"

I sat down at my desk and got to it right away, recreating our conversation as you see it above. I typed the last sentence and looked at it for a long moment, wondering if I had anything further to add. I decided that I didn't, and had just closed the file when there was a knock on the door.

I looked at my watch. He'd given me a full hour.

I told him to come in, pointed to a chair. It's a comfortable chair, but he didn't look all that comfortable in it. And I could understand that. I'd already provided an unbidden confession to homicide. Who could say what I might come up with next?

"You probably have some questions," I said.

He shrugged.

"Like why did I decide to tell you all this."

"I guess I wondered."

"I never expected to. When I started driving east, I'd

reached a point where it was beginning to look as though I might get away with it. By the time I got to Ohio I had a new name and some ID to go with it. I began to create a completely new life for myself, and I figured the past could stay in the past."

"But then with DNA—"

"Not just DNA. The whole business of cold case investigation. The world's changing at a pace that makes your head spin, and one big change is that there's no getting away from the past. It's right there in the present."

"I'm not sure I understand."

"If you go back, oh, say a hundred years ago. No, make it a little more than that. A hundred and fifty years, say. All the way back to the days of the Old West. Think of those movies and TV shows that open with a guy on a horse, riding across the prairie and into town. Whatever past he may have had, he could just leave it behind—in some other town.

"His name was whatever he called himself. Nobody could ask to see a man's ID, because he didn't have any and neither did anybody else. Your story was whatever you said it was, and unless somebody from your past rode into town, you could live your new life and forget about your old one."

He was nodding, getting the picture. "No security cameras," he said.

"They were pretty scarce as recently as twenty years ago. Liquor stores and other retailers in high-crime areas had them, but they didn't work all that well, and people would forget to maintain them. Porter Dawes had one, just a single camera aimed at the checkout counter, and one of my duties was rewinding the tape at closing time and setting it up for the next day. Now we've got four cameras inside the store and one outside, and they're digital and they pretty much maintain themselves. And that's in a store that's never been held up even once."

We talked about the cameras, and what deterrent value they might have for potential shoplifters. As far as robbery went, we were an unlikely target in the first place, and became less of one each year, as our proportion of credit card sales increased.

We'd wandered off the subject, but that was all right. A father and son, enjoying the back-and-forth of a conversation. When it had run its course, or at least as much of its course as it needed to run, I said, "You didn't expect all this when you started to tell me about my brother Hank."

"I don't know what I expected, Dad."

"But not this conversation."

"No, I guess not."

"Neither did I. I wanted that whole part of my life to stay in Bakersfield."

"That's where it happened?"

"And that's where I'd come to believe I'd left it. Like that cowboy, riding into town and starting over. I've been living that new life for all these years, to the point where I barely remember the old life, and the man I used to be."

"Buddy," he said.

"Buddy's gone," I said, "and it's not hard to let myself believe he never really existed in the first place. I didn't think anyone would find a way to follow his trail all the way east to Ohio. And I didn't think anyone here would ever have to know anything about what happened back there."

He thought about that, took it in, nodded.

"When forensic analysis improved, when the whole business of cold case investigation started making headlines and showing up on TV, what bothered me most wasn't the prospect of a trial and a prison sentence. It was that you and your mother would know who I was and what I'd done."

"Mom doesn't know any of this."

"No. But you'd both find out in a hurry if they came knocking on the door. And your sister, too, and I can't even wrap my mind around that."

"No."

I closed my eyes for a moment, picked my words carefully. I said, "It was hard to have this conversation. But it kept getting harder *not* to have it."

"I think I know what you mean."

"One thing that bothered me, and I don't even know how conscious I was of it, but in order to keep this particular secret, I had to consign all of my past life to the shadows. There were all these things about me that I couldn't let you know. For God's sake, I have nine brothers and sisters! That's nine aunts and uncles that you were never going to know about. I won't pretend we were close, but they existed, and you had a right to know about them, and I couldn't tell you. Of course they're not blood kin of yours, but—"

"They might as well be," he said. "You're my dad, they're your brothers and sisters, so that makes them my uncles and aunts. And I don't even know how much blood matters, but it's a fact that they're blood kin to Kristy."

"Yes, that's true."

"DNA and all," he said.

DNA and all.

I felt better for our conversation, I told him. It had relieved me of some inner tension. We talked a little more, and then he went off to do homework and I sat down and recorded our conversation.

YOU'RE MY DAD. Three words, uttered with no particular inflection, yet they'd put a lump in my throat and kept coming back to me.

And indeed I am. And Kristin's dad as well, and Louella's husband. I'm J. J. Thompson, long-established local retailer, member of various civic-minded fraternal organizations. Infrequent churchgoer, once-a-week bowler. A family man. A man, as I believe I've already called myself, of settled habits.

I'm all those things. I'm also Buddy, and Roger before that.

"You're my dad."

I type the words and I can hear him saying them, and they continue to move me. And they bring to mind another three-word statement which they seem to echo:

"I forgive you."

And I find myself at the brink of tears. But I don't have to hold them back. They hold themselves back.

I WROTE THE previous entry four days ago. Shut down the computer, went downstairs, and went on with my life. The following day I never even walked into my office, and the day after that I found myself thinking that this journal (if I want to call it that, and I suppose it's as good a word as any)—that this journal had served a purpose and been a valuable outlet, but that its time had come and gone and now I was done with it.

Perhaps I ought to delete the file. Or, because deletion is such an uncertain and inconclusive process, perhaps what I really ought to do is junk the computer after having destroyed its hard drive.

It's probably due for a replacement, anyway. I don't know how many years I've owned it, but certainly two or three years longer than I've owned my car. Every two or three years a man will spend money on a car that's not substantially different from the one he's trading in; computers, meanwhile, evolve far more rapidly, yet we keep them as long as we can.

And I've had this thought, and will doubtless have it again, and I'll keep this laptop (which wouldn't dream of complaining even as I peck away at its keys) until it breaks down and makes the decision for me.

As I said, it's been four days. And it might have been several more, there's no way of guessing how long it might have been, but for the show that aired tonight on *Dateline*.

A cold case solved. A woman in eastern Tennessee, not far from Knoxville, who'd laced up her Nikes and gone for a run eighteen years ago.

And never came home.

There'd been the usual reports, sightings from as far away as Denver, but they never panned out. She was presumed dead, and likely buried, tucked deep in some patch of earth where she wouldn't be found.

They were fairly sure it was the husband, and it didn't help his cause when he flunked a polygraph test. But he'd stayed with his story—she went out, she didn't come back, I got no idea where she went to—and polygraph results aren't admissible evidence. The local DA decided they didn't have enough of a case to take to court, and if they'd tried, a defense attorney could have pointed out that she had a sort-of boyfriend, her occasional running partner, and while both his alibi and his own polygraph results had cleared him as far as the police were concerned, his role in her life might be enough to a jury to constitute an alternate theory of the crime, leading to reasonable doubt.

And there was no body. You always needed a much stronger case when you didn't have a body to point to.

So the husband was never charged, let alone convicted, but everybody thought he'd done it, his kids included, and within a year he'd sold up and relocated to Baton Rouge. He moved a few more times over the years, and by the time they found the body he was in a halfway house in Medford, Oregon, fresh out of his latest stint of rehab and working in a car wash.

It was an old man with a metal detector who found her. After a lifetime of teaching history at the University of Tennessee, he'd settled on two hobbies to enliven his retirement. He foraged for edible wild plants, and while he gathered them he scanned the ground with a metal detector, turning up musket balls and stray coins and no end of rings from pop-top beer cans.

The woman—I could let Google supply her name, but what difference does it make? Although she'd been buried with her wedding ring on her finger, it seems unlikely that would have been enough to set his device humming. But she'd broken a femur some years back, and the repair of the fracture had entailed implanting a metal rod, and, well, you get the picture.

He started digging, and when he began finding bones he picked up his phone and called it in.

They went to Oregon to pick up the husband, who'd needed a minute to figure out what wife they were talking about; he'd been married and divorced twice since then, and opioid use had left him a little vague. Yes, he confirmed, they'd inserted a metal rod when they fixed her leg, and if it was titanium it was probably worth a couple of dollars, and he supposed it was nice that they found her, but it still had nothing to do with him. Wasn't him that killed her, or dug a hole and left her in it.

And, remarkably, he was right about that. While they were checking DNA to make sure it was in fact the running lady they'd found, they came across some other DNA and figured it was the husband's, which would wrap up the case against him and tie a bow on it.

Nope. It was the boyfriend's. His wife had divorced him early on, and he'd left her with the house and kids and moved to East Texas. He'd remarried and had two more children, he'd set himself up again as an optometrist, he mowed his lawn and kept up with his garden, he coached his younger daughter's soccer team—and he hadn't seemed at all surprised when they came knocking on his door. The case against him was way short of being a slam-dunk, but he invited the officers in and poured them glasses of iced tea and told them everything. Waived extradition, accompanied them voluntarily to Knox County to await trial, where on advice of counsel he repudiated his confession, withdrew his initial Guilty plea, and wound up backing his way into a life sentence.

While the story was unfolding, I waited for some relative's DNA from *23 and Me* to kickstart the cold case, because nowadays that's always what I'm waiting for. But that never had a chance to play a role; they'd had both men's DNA on file all along, the innocent husband and the guilty boyfriend, and all they had to do was run the usual tests. They did, and that was that.

But this case resonated in another way entirely. If there's a God, it shows him to be the Supreme Ironist. Here you've got two men, the husband and the boyfriend, and both their lives take the path you'd pretty much expect them to take. The husband, clearly guilty despite the legal presumption of innocence, had gone downhill in a hurry, stumbling almost inevitably into alcoholism and opioid addiction, with a good chance of dying of an overdose when his latest stint in rehab proved no more enduring than the ones preceding it. Unpunished by the law, perhaps, but punished by life.

Meanwhile the boyfriend, presumed innocent not only by the legal system but by all concerned, had shrugged off the breakup of his marriage and created an exemplary new life for himself. He'd been genuinely successful, not merely in his profession but as a husband and father. You can make of it what you will, but his daughter's soccer team hadn't lost a match all season.

And he was the one who was guilty, and who'd be spending the rest of his life in prison—while his new wife and kids tried to come to terms with the turn their lives had taken.

You might say it got my attention.

I came up here to write about it, and didn't stop to wonder why I felt the need to do so. Nothing *Dateline* had to report changes my situation in any way that I can see. But the story has had an impact, which probably shouldn't be surprising, and sitting here and tapping keys and forming words and sentences on the screen seems to be the way I've found for processing the thoughts in my mind and the events in my life. I don't know that it helps me to put things in perspective, whatever that means, but it's what I've taught myself to do, and I suspect I do it for a reason.

I wonder what Alden made of it.

We'd all four sat down to watch the show, but fifteen minutes in Kristin yawned theatrically and went to her room to play a video game. Louella wandered into the kitchen from time to time, she had something in the oven that required her occasional attention, but Alden and I never stirred from our seats.

Now and then I'd glance over at him, and a couple of times our eyes met. I don't know what he was thinking, but I could probably guess.

ALDEN WADE SHIPLEY Thompson.

He was a young man, but he was also a boy, and what a load I'd given him to carry. Had I been right or wrong to share my secret with him?

The answer would be easier to furnish if I knew for certain how much would ever be known about the death of Cindy Raschmann. Would a pair of cops from California come knocking on our door?

It was one thing if they did, another if they didn't.

And they might not. Investigations stall out. A case that had been so cold for so many years might never warm up enough to lead anywhere. There was no telling how good their DNA sample had been, or how much it might have degraded over the years. Or if they'd misplaced the damned thing, and given up looking for it.

And state and local governments were increasingly handicapped by budget cuts, and I would think they'd have to practice a sort of triage in cold case investigations, allocating resources to the ones they had the best chance of resolving—or with the higher profiles, or those in which the victim's next of kin made the most insistent demands for closure.

Closure. That's right up there with *perspective.* I don't know what the hell it means.

And one hears it all the time. "I had to stay with the case," a dogged lawman will tell the camera, "because I felt it was my job to bring those good people closure."

And, when they presumably have achieved it, when the guilty verdict comes down and the sentence is read and the killer led off to spend the rest of his life in prison, where's the closure? Aside from a measure of mean-spirited satisfaction, what those friends and relatives give off most is a sense of disappointment.

She's still dead. Life goes on, and so does death, and now what? Is that all there is?

IF THEY CAME for me, the conversation I'd had with Alden would take a little of the shock and horror out of what followed. He'd be able to comfort his mother, to reassure his sister.

And if they never did show up?

I STOPPED THERE, slept on the question, woke up with what

feels like the answer. Perhaps a night's sleep has given me a measure of perspective, if not closure.

I'm closer to Alden for our having had that conversation, for his knowing the awful truth about the man who has become his father. If the case of Cindy Raschmann remains cold forever, if the most unsettling visitors ever to ring our doorbell are Jehovah's Witnesses and cookie-peddling Girl Scouts, there's still more good than bad in having revealed myself to my son.

No closure here, I'm afraid. I've managed to answer one question only to raise another.

THAT LAST ENTRY was made the day before yesterday, typed out quickly before I went down for breakfast.

The forecast was for rain, so I drove to Thompson Dawes, and caught the news on the radio. An item drew my attention as I was pulling into my parking space, and I stayed put long enough to hear it through to the end.

It concerned a man in Missouri who'd been doing twenty years to life in a state penitentiary for killing a woman. There was no new evidence, and couldn't be; the crime had been witnessed, the physical evidence supported the conviction, and he'd confessed immediately and never tried to repudiate the confession.

Six months ago a judge had ordered his release. The prisoner was 76 years old, and had spent almost half his life in a cell, and had reached an age where he was certainly no threat to society.

So they let him go, and in less than six months the son of a bitch did it again. Got himself a hunting knife, the sort you'd use to skin out a deer, and killed a middle-aged woman with a single stab wound to the heart. She was, as far as anyone could determine, a stranger to him, and if he had a motive he'd thus far kept it to himself.

All morning long I kept thinking of all concerned—the man himself, the two women he'd killed some forty years apart, and the judge whose re-election now seemed unlikely.

What did it mean? And why did it seem to possess some significance, still annoyingly unclear, for me?

It never did rain.

THAT WAS YESTERDAY.

Woke up this morning to a clear day, cool but not cold. I took the car because I'd need to drive to a lunchtime meeting, but I'd already pretty much decided to skip it, and at noon when I got behind the wheel I didn't even think about heading downtown.

I hadn't been aware of making a decision, hadn't gone to sleep with the conscious hope that I'd wake up with an answer. But evidently a decision had made itself, and an unasked question had been answered.

I drove home. The garage was empty, so Louella had gone somewhere.

A supermarket visit? Probably.

I went to the living room, turned the TV on and off again, picked up a magazine. I paged through it, and it wasn't long before I heard her car in the driveway. By the time I got outside she had the trunk open and was lifting a bag of groceries. I took it from her, and she drew a second bag out of the trunk, and I followed her inside.

"Well, this is a surprise," she said. "I thought you had Kiwanis today."

"They can get along without me."

"While I," she said, "cannot."

We kissed, and she stepped back and looked at me. Her expression of mild puzzlement was understandable. I was very much a creature of habits, and coming home at noon, unannounced and for no particular reason, was not one of them.

But she was not alarmed. Whatever had brought me home, she could wait for it to reveal itself.

I said, "I was a little concerned about you."

"About me?"

"This morning, before I left the house."

"At breakfast?"

"Your energy level," I said. "Have you been feeling all right?"

"I'm fine," she said. "At least I thought I was fine, until you raised the subject just now. What exactly—"

"You just seem very tired to me," I said. "Sleepy, even."

"Sleepy."

"As if you didn't get enough sleep last night, and now you can barely keep your eyes open."

Her face softened, her eyes brightened. "Now that you mention it—"

"You're tired, aren't you?"

"Exhausted," she said, "and isn't it funny how I wasn't even aware of it myself?"

"Well, sometimes it's easier for another person to spot these things."

"That must be it."

"Especially when it's another person who knows you very well."

"Almost better than I know myself," she said. "My goodness, here I am, as tired as I've ever been. I really ought to be in bed."

"You really should."

"And here you are," she said, moving to the staircase. "Home for lunch."

"Isn't it funny how things work out?"

"Oh, it is," she said. "It is indeed."

"OH MY," SHE said, a while later.

"Feel better now?"

Her answer was a low chuckle.

"I guess you needed that nap."

"And I guess your lunch was worth the drive home. Or did you walk? No, you took the car."

"I had the car," I said, "but my lunch would have been worth it if I walked. Or even if I crawled on my belly like a reptile."

That put her in mind of measuring worms, and their curious manner of locomotion, and we both remembered something we'd seen on TV, some penitent Asian monk who made his way to some sacred shrine in a manner which could only have been inspired by a measuring worm. We speculated on what sort of sin could inspire such a performance, and why this had seemed to him to be a reasonable way to expiate it. And then the conversation wandered here and there, in a less systematic fashion than either the monk or the measuring worm might have chosen.

Among other things, I told her I loved her, and she said she loved me. And she yawned and stretched and said, as each of us has remarked often over the years, how very lucky we were to have found each other.

I said, "I hope you still feel that way at the day's end."

"I'll probably still be glowing," she said, and then my words registered and her face showed concern.

"There's a conversation we need to have," I told her.

She sat up. "Are you all right? Darling, should I call a doctor?"

Not a doctor, I thought. Maybe a lawyer.

What I said was, "No, I'm fine. But there are things I need to tell you, and I don't know where to begin."

AND THAT'S HOW I got started, by confessing that I wasn't sure where to begin, or how. That may have been as good a way as any. It got the words flowing.

It's not important what words I found or what order I put them in. At the onset I would hear the words first in my head, so that I could choose what to say and what to leave unsaid, but it wasn't long before that little echo-in-advance went silent, and I just went ahead and said what I had to say.

I talked for a long time, although I couldn't say how long. I didn't note the time I got started, and I wasn't really conscious of time throughout. I was sitting up in bed beside her when I began, and I never changed position. Nor did she, stretched out on her side next to me. I would glance at her from time to time, but mostly my eyes, focused on nothing in particular, were aimed at the foot of the bed.

Where Cindy Raschmann had been standing when she told me I was forgiven.

When I did look at Louella, I couldn't read much of anything in her expression. She appeared attentive throughout, and when I paused so that she could offer a comment or a question, she supplied neither, simply waiting for me to continue.

I wondered at this. Over the years I've a couple of times been called upon to give a talk to one of my groups, and I've learned to draw energy from my audience, seeking out with my eyes those visibly receptive listeners whose nods and facial expressions urge me along like a silent amen chorus. I wasn't getting any of that now, as I sought the understanding and acceptance of the most important audience I'd ever addressed.

But I can see now that she gave me throughout my performance precisely the response I required. She listened, she paid close attention, she took it all in—and she gave me the space to go on.

And what did I say? What did I withhold?

You'd think I'd remember it all word for word, or close to it. But I don't, and I'm hard put to explain why.

What matters, I suppose, is that I uttered the words, not that my recollection of them is imperfect.

I know I talked far more than I'd expected to about my childhood and my family. It was unusual for me to think much about those years, although Alden's reports on Kristin's long-lost second cousins did spark memories. Two of my older brothers, one teasing the other about a girl. A sister, curiously incapable of learning how to ride a two-wheel bicycle, then just as curiously mastering the whole business in a couple of hours.

This and that . . .

I PAUSED JUST now and scrolled up to read the account I've written of the murder I committed, and of the pleasure I took in it and in the sexual performance that followed it. My recital this afternoon was less detailed.

I suppose that's only natural. One wants to be honest and forthcoming, but one balks at revealing oneself to be a monster.

WHEN I STOPPED, when I had finally run out of words, she acknowledged that I was done talking by laying her hand lightly upon mine. The warm touch of her fingers on the back of my hand moved me beyond words.

"I'm glad you told me," she said, "and not the Rotary Club."

Kiwanis, I thought.

"I mean Kiwanis," she said, as if I'd spoken the word aloud. "You came home so that you could tell me."

"Yes."

"But first you made love to me."

"Yes."

She didn't say anything, so I answered the question she hadn't asked.

"I thought it might be our last time," I said. "Once you knew the truth—"

"I'd be horrified? Sickened?"

"Are you?"

She took time to think about it. "I knew there was something," she said. "Each of us had a life before we found each

other, and that's fine, nobody needs to know every last detail
about anybody else. I had an uncle who molested me. I never
told you that."

"No."

"I was really little. Like five or six. Can you imagine wanting to have sex with someone that age? A little child?"

"No."

"It happened twice. He said he had something to show me,
and that I would like it, and what he did was take down my
panties and lick me. For, I don't know, a few minutes. Then he
stopped and pulled my panties back up again and pulled my
skirt down and told me I was a wonderful beautiful little girl
and I must never say a word to anybody about what we'd just
done. And I never did."

"Until now."

"Until now. And I still haven't told you the worst part of
all. *I liked it.*"

"You weren't frightened?"

"I probably should have been, but it never occurred to me.
I just loved the way it felt. In fact I adored it. What?"

"What?"

"The expression on your face."

"Oh," I said. "What I was thinking—"

"I know what you were thinking. 'You still do.' "

"Well?"

She took a deliberate breath. "The second time," she said,
"must have been two or three weeks later. Maybe more. I
wonder why he waited so long."

"Could have been guilt," I suggested. "Or fear, or a

combination of the two. He'd done something awful, and as long as you kept quiet he'd get away with it, and now he had to make sure it never happened again."

"And then he looked at me and found me utterly irresistible?"

"Something like that."

"I wonder. Anyway, the two of us were alone, and he asked me if I'd like to have some fun. And of course I knew what he meant. And I sat on the couch next to him, and my skirt went up and my panties came down and this time I didn't have to wonder what was going on, or decide how I felt about it."

"And you still liked it?"

"Oh, God, I loved it. I don't think I had an orgasm. Is it possible for a girl that age to have an orgasm?"

"I'm afraid that's outside my area of expertise."

"I think it's possible, because I think if he'd kept it up a few more minutes I would have had one then and there. But I guess he had one of his own, because he trembled and made this moaning sound, and before I knew it I had my panties on again and he was telling me what he'd told me the first time. How wonderful I was, and how this had to be our little secret."

"And there was no third time?"

"No, and I was waiting for it. I didn't really think much about it after the first time. It happened and I liked it, but I didn't even think enough about it to wonder if it would happen again. But after the second time, well, I thought about it a lot. In fact I would be thinking about it and I would touch myself."

"And imagine your finger was Uncle Don?"

"Uncle Howie. His name was Howard Desmond, he was married to my Aunt Pauline. My father had two sisters, both of them younger than himself, and Aunt Pauline was the younger of the two. I don't know what I was thinking about when I touched myself. It just felt good and I liked making myself feel good."

"And Uncle Howie—"

"Died."

"Oh."

"He was driving and he lost control of the car. I was too young to go to the funeral. I wonder how old a child has to be to go to a funeral. I suppose it varies from family to family, and it depends how close you were to the deceased."

"And you were closer than anybody realized."

"I wonder," she said, "if anybody knew anything. Maybe I wasn't the first little girl Uncle Howie mistook for an ice cream cone. And you know what else I wonder? It was, I don't know, just a few years ago, that somebody on TV was talking about unwitnessed single-car accidents, and how they're a way to commit suicide and get away with it."

"If you're dead, how exactly are you getting away with it?"

"The stigma. Or insurance, where they wouldn't pay if they could prove you killed yourself."

"That's what people think," I said. "That suicide invalidates an insurance claim, but that's hardly ever the case if a policy's been in force for a certain amount of time. After a year or two, it won't get them off the hook."

"I didn't know that."

"But you're thinking your uncle killed himself."

"When he supposedly lost control of the car," she said, "he ran it into one of the concrete pillars supporting the Lyons Avenue overpass. 'That's where your Uncle Howie had his accident.' I remember hearing that more than once when I was in a car and we were driving past where it happened. And maybe it was an accident, because people do lose control of their cars and drive into things like bridge abutments, but if nobody was there to see him do it, it's like that tree in the forest."

"The one that fell without making a sound."

"That's the one. Once the possibility occurred to me, and this was years and years after the fact—"

"When you heard something on TV."

"Right. Were the grownups in the family wondering about this all along? There's nobody to ask, they're all long gone. No way to know if it was really an accident. Or if it was half an accident, if he'd had a few drinks and was driving too fast and has this sudden impulse and swung the steering wheel hard right."

"And stomped the accelerator instead of the brake."

" 'Oh, the hell with it.' Like that, maybe."

"And what you're really wondering," I said, "is what if anything you had to do with it."

"If he did it on purpose, it could have been anything. Fear of exposure. Fear of what he might do next. Hating himself for what he was. I mean, there's no way of knowing."

"No."

"People suffer from depression. It doesn't necessarily have

anything to do with what's going on in their lives. I don't feel guilty about it, because I didn't do anything. I honestly don't blame myself."

"Good, because you shouldn't."

"But I wonder," she said, "about what would have happened if he'd kept the car on the road. I'll tell you one thing that did happen. I stopped thinking about what we did. Or what he did, I guess I should say. You know, skirt up, panties down."

"Tongue extended."

She rolled her eyes. "I didn't think about it. It had to do with Uncle Howie, and he was gone forever, and I would never see him again. And that was sad, so the thing to do was to stop thinking of him. I sort of forgot about it, and I even forgot to touch myself, at least for a while. I, uh, rediscovered that part later."

"What a hot little girl you were."

"Oh, not really. You want to know something? Nobody ever did that to me again until—"

"Until what? Until you were married? Until you ran into Martina Navratilova at that bar on Railroad Avenue?"

"Idiot. Until I went out to buy a pressure cooker and wound up with the man of my dreams."

"But you'd been married."

"And it wasn't a bad marriage, and Duane and I had an okay time in bed, but oral sex was never a part of it. He never initiated it and I never thought about it."

"You never thought about it."

"I honestly didn't. I was a little kid when it happened, and

I walled it off in my mind and forgot about it. I certainly never had the thought *Oh now that I'm married I can do what I did with Uncle Howie.*" She frowned. "I suppose it must have been traumatic, but it never felt that way."

"And you never told anybody."

"Well, he said not to, didn't he? And what about you? You never said anything."

"Until now."

"You told Alden. It's funny, when the two of you came home the other night I knew there was something that happened. I thought maybe you'd had one of those talks where you tell him to always wear a condom. You know, fatherly advice. Guy stuff."

"Not exactly."

And I said that I'd given Alden an edited version of my history, shorter and less detailed. But wasn't what she'd just heard itself an edited version? I hadn't supplied every thought that went through my mind, every impulse, every feeling. I'd recounted a great deal of what I've recorded in this unending electronic document, but by no means all of it.

And hasn't this document itself had the services of an internal but always present editor? Don't I choose what to put down and what to leave out?

WE TALKED FOR a long time. At one point she got up and showered, and when she'd finished I took her place in the shower, and we put on clothes and went down to the kitchen and ate sandwiches and drank coffee and talked some more.

A lot of it was speculation. What might happen, and how likely it was, and how we could respond to one or another scenario. Thoughts arose, and we chased them down and examined them.

There were times, too, when the conversation would stop. Shared silences.

"I never knew you owned a gun," she said.

"How would you know? It's tucked away in a locked drawer."

"Promise me you'll never use it."

I'd told her I'd thought of it as a last-ditch emergency exit, a way out if there was no other way out. When the men from Bakersfield climbed onto the porch and knocked on the door, I could put the gun to my head and spare myself what otherwise would follow.

I hadn't told her another way I'd imagined myself using the gun, stalking from room to room, sparing us all the pain of exposure, not only myself but her and Alden and Kristin. The inner editor was on the job, and I was grateful for it. It was almost impossible now, sitting over cups of coffee, to imagine I had ever entertained such a thought, and it was one that never needed to be shared.

"I'll never use it," I said. "It can stay where it is, locked away in its drawer, doing no harm to anyone. And to hell with Chekhov."

CHEKHOV PUZZLED HER, until I explained the reference. She agreed the revolver could stay locked away forever. It didn't need to be fired before the final curtain.

"SO YOUR NAME was originally—" She broke off the sentence, held up a hand. "No, don't tell me, because I'm going to let myself forget it. It's not your name. Your name is John James Thompson, and that's who you are. That's the name of the man I fell in love with and married and had a baby with, and I'm Louella Thompson, *Mrs.* John James Thompson, and that's all we need to know about names. John, I love you more than ever."

"And I you."

"And I am so glad we had this conversation. I always told myself that you and I could tell each other anything and it would be all right. And it's more than all right, isn't it? I feel closer to you than ever." She looked away for a moment. "Sooner or later," she said, "we'll have to tell Kristin."

"But not yet."

"No, it would be way too much for her to process. At least I think it would. Or she might just roll her eyes. 'Like I didn't already *know* that, Mom.' "

"God, I can hear her saying it. But with a question mark at the end."

"Just a trace of Valley Girl." She drew a breath. "We'll know when it's time, and how to tell her what she needs to know."

"Yes."

"And whatever happens," she said, "we'll get through this."

* * *

I'VE SAT DOWN at the computer a couple of times over the last month, but the need to add words and sentences to this document seems to have subsided.

I'm sure it's a result of those two conversations, first with Alden and then with Louella. I spent some months writing down secrets, things I'd thought and imagined and done about which I could never tell anyone. And then, having shared my secrets with the two most important people in my life, I no longer needed to share them with my hard drive.

Still, habits want to persist. On a few occasions I would find myself sitting here, where I'd write down a sentence or two only to erase it—not because it needed to be erased, but because it had never needed to be written in the first place. Then long moments, some spent reading over what I'd written, some spent doing nothing at all, and then a few words or a sentence, and then I'd erase that, too, and eventually I'd close the file and shut off the computer and go back downstairs.

But it seems to me I should make note of what happened this evening. I was in the living room reading a magazine; we'd watched *Jeopardy,* and after we all answered the Final Jeopardy question (or supplied a question for the Final Jeopardy answer), Louella and Kristin settled in with whatever was on HGTV. Alden gave me a significant look, and I put down my magazine and followed him onto the porch, where he told me he couldn't be 100% positive, but he thought he'd managed to remove his sister's DNA from the agency's database.

"Maybe not remove it," he said, "because nowadays I don't think anybody can ever remove anything, and pretty soon they'll stop bothering to put DELETE keys on computers. But I think I fixed it so nobody can get access to it. Like if somebody submits his DNA and they look for matches and near matches, the way they do, well, they won't find out what genes they share with Kristin."

How had he managed that?

"I'm not positive I did," he said, "because to find out for sure I'd have to figure out a way to test it, and how do I do that and make sure I'm not raising any red flags in the process? But what I did, I got a lawyer to call them and say how she was a minor, and her DNA was submitted without her permission or the permission of her lawful guardian. So they were on notice not to communicate with her in any manner, or to provide information about her DNA profile to anyone, or even to keep her genetic information on file. What's the matter?"

"The lawyer," I said. "Who did you use?"

"Edward P. Hammerschmidt."

"How much did you have to tell him?"

"Uh, I didn't tell him anything."

"Well, you must have," I said. "You couldn't just write out a script for him. How would he know what to say? And how could he keep from wondering what kind of a secret we had to be sitting on? And—"

"Dad."

"And where the hell did you find him, anyway? I can't claim to know every lawyer in Allen County, but Hammerschmidt's a name I'd recognize if I'd ever come across it before, and I didn't, so—"

"Dad?"

I looked up.

"Dad, I made him up. I got this DNA guy on the phone, I forget his name, and I said I was Edward P. Hammerschmidt, attorney in fact for the legal guardian of a minor child, and, well, I rattled it off."

"And he bought it?" I thought about it. "Well," I said, "why wouldn't he?"

"That's what I figured."

"Easy enough to comply with your request and avoid whatever action you might take. That doesn't mean the data will completely disappear from their system."

"There's probably no way to make that happen. I mean, even if that's what he tried to do, would he even be able to do it? A hundred percent?"

"Seems unlikely."

"It'd be like if somebody tells you to forget something ever happened. People say that all the time, but nobody expects you to erase something from your memory, because how could you even do that? 'Okay, I'll forget I saw Mommy kissing Santa Claus.' But if nobody can access Kristy's data, and if nobody gets emails saying there's a young girl in Ohio who's a probable second cousin—"

"Then it's as good as erased."

"Maybe," he said. "Anyway, I figured it was worth a shot."

HE IS, AS I've noted before, a resourceful young man, and no one could wish for a better son. It's impossible to calculate percentages, but I'm confident that his five-minute phone call has improved my chances.

I feel safer now, I was about to write (and in fact did write it, in this very sentence, but never mind). But is it so? I'm aware that I'm more likely to escape detection than I was before he passed himself off as Edward P. Hammerschmidt, Esq. But knowing isn't feeling, so the question arises: Do I feel any safer now?

And here's what I've just realized: I don't feel any safer, because I don't need an increased feeling of safety—and that's because I haven't felt myself to be in any genuine peril ever since those two conversations, first with Alden and then with Louella.

They didn't render me any safer. They didn't lessen the likelihood that a cold case in Bakersfield would warm up and reach all the way to Lima.

But what they succeeded in doing was making me *feel* safe. There's a sense now that nothing can really touch me, that the people who matter in my life—and matter so much more than I ever thought anyone could matter—that they know all my secrets, and love me as much as they ever did.

As much? Arguably more. The husband and father they know is less armored, less hidden.

And if the secret they now know is monstrous, it doesn't seem to have led them to regard me as a monster. I may have done something monstrous, I may even be said to have gone through a Monster Phase, but—

"But that was in another country. And besides, the wench is dead."

The line is Christopher Marlowe's, from *The Jew of Malta,* a play I've neither seen nor read. I've no idea where I came across it, though I could probably guess why it stuck in my mind sufficiently to make me Google it just now. The speaker's crime was fornication, surely a lesser offense than homicide, but the similarities are undeniable. It was indeed in another state, if not another country. And, yes, God rest her soul—the wench is dead.

I'd told Louella that I'd made love to her in advance of our conversation because I thought it might be for the last time. Even if she accepted what I was about to tell her, even if we stood together as husband and wife and went on sharing a bedroom, it seemed possible that her new knowledge would rule out physical intimacy.

But it wasn't more than a day or two after our conversation that she yawned theatrically and announced that she could barely keep her eyes open. On that occasion, and twice since then, what she now knew did nothing to diminish her ardor and enthusiasm.

And who knows, really, what else she brings to the bed-chamber? She knows I killed a woman, and to be comfortable in my embrace she has to wall off that knowledge in some chamber of her memory.

But how impermeable is that wall? Perhaps she leaves an opening, perhaps she allows herself now and then to rub up against what she knows. Perhaps her passion is heightened by imagining what I might do—while knowing that I won't.

Isn't that why people go to horror movies? So that they can relish the thrill of fear in an unthreatening environment? What's on the screen scares them, but does so in a safe way. It's an illusion, up there on the screen, and they're in the audience with a bag of popcorn, or at home on the couch with the re-mote control in their hands.

And doesn't that help explain the audience for true crime shows? There are a couple of cable channels devoted exclu-sively to them, while the broadcast networks keep pumping out *Dateline* and *48 Hours*. The abiding majority of cases feature women as victims, which may not come as a surprise, but here's something I only recently learned, and did find surprising: the audience for these programs is predominantly female.

On the screen, it's a woman who gets herself shot or stabbed or strangled. And it's a man who does the killing, and the husband or boyfriend is almost always a suspect, and more often than not he's guilty.

And the woman watching can hardly escape thinking of her own man. He's in his basement workshop trimming out a model plane, or in his den with his stamp collection. Or walking the family dog, or having a beer with his buddies.

And he would never do anything like the husband on the television screen.

Would he?

Maybe that's part of it. And, if it is, what business is it of mine?

I can't know everything that's going on in her mind, her heart, her deepest self. Nor can she know all my innermost secrets, the deepest of which I'm sure are unknown even to me.

"I'm so sleepy," she'll say, with something that is not quite a twinkle in her eye. "I think you should get some rest," I'll respond.

And, while we become as close as two human beings can possibly be, each of us is off somewhere, listening to some personal music that no one else can ever hear.

A DECISION THIS afternoon, not unexpected, from Alden. He'll be starting college in September at Ohio State's Lima campus. That means he can live at home. In fact it's a virtual necessity, as OSU-Lima doesn't have dormitories.

He had applied, at his guidance counselor's urging, to five schools, and was accepted at all of them. The only strong contender, beside OSU-Lima, was the university's main campus in Columbus. That's where he'll almost certainly go to vet school, and there he'd have the traditional college life of football games and fraternities and pep rallies and beer blasts, or as much of it as still exists these days.

I thought he might want all that, thought too that he'd get a better undergraduate education at Columbus than the local school could offer. And he would indeed have a richer menu of courses to choose from, and a more illustrious faculty, but he's sure OSU-Lima will get him into grad school at Columbus, and that's all he wants from it.

I'd be paying a few thousand dollars a year less for his tuition this way, he pointed out, and of course I'd be saving money on dorm fees and meals, plus he'd get to eat his mother's cooking instead of whatever mystery meat they served up in the school cafeteria.

But the biggest factor was his apprenticeship with Ralph, which could continue during his four undergraduate years. "By the time I finish," he said, "I'll probably be more qualified than most vet school graduates. In fact Ralph says I should be able to fit in some original research while I'm at Columbus. Not that you'd need that on your résumé in order to give rabies shots, but I think it'd be cool."

And wasn't he concerned that he might be missing something?

"What, like in *Animal House*? Come on."

So he'll be here, under our roof, and the money his decision will save me, while certainly welcome, is nothing compared to the pleasure of having him here for the next four years.

Best of all is knowing that this is what he wants, that he'd rather stay in Lima than move a hundred miles east to the

state capital. That he'd rather live at home. With his mother
and sister. And me.

And it wasn't hard to figure out what to get him in June.

"Besides," he'd said at one point, "if I did go to Columbus,
you know I'd be coming home one or two weekends a month.
That's a couple of hours wasted each way, plus the cost of the
gas. And there's the wear and tear on the Subaru. I mean it's
okay here in town, you know, but I don't know how long it'll
hold up, you know?"

I'm already looking forward to the two of us on a joint
mission to pick out his graduation present.

I JUST LOOKED at the most recent entry. Before I write what
I came upstairs to write, I feel compelled to note that Alden
and I shopped around shortly before the principal handed
him his high school diploma, and he's now driving a new
steel-blue Hyundai Elantra.

"Are you sure, Dad? Brand new? I figured, you know, pre-
owned."

I told him I was afraid he'd have to do the pre-owning, for
whoever might buy it after he'd traded it in.

"No way," he said, patting a fender. "I'm keeping this baby
forever."

AND WHAT HE said an hour or so ago was, "Whoever that guy's supposed to be, he doesn't look like anybody I've ever seen."

He was referring to two black-and-white photographs, both of the same subject. The first showed a teenage male, looking uncomfortable in a plaid jacket and a striped tie, a rigid half-smile on his face. The second looked at first to be a picture of the boy's father, but it was in fact the youth himself, transformed through some combination of artistic license and computer magic into a middle-aged man.

He was still wearing the jacket and tie, but both garments had been altered—updated, I suppose. Each had lost its pattern, so that he appeared to be wearing a blazer and a dark tie. One's imagination colored the new image—a navy blazer, a maroon necktie.

His hairline was higher, his brow lined, his features showing the years. One thing that hadn't changed was his facial expression. He still looked posed and uncomfortable, and as if he'd have preferred to be standing almost anywhere other than in front of this camera. That sort of expression and attitude was somehow better suited to an adolescent than to a mature man, but I don't suppose a computer could be readily programmed to give instructions to the subject of a doctored photograph: "*Grow up, sonny. Get over yourself.*"

"Breaking news," Lester Holt had said, as he almost invariably does as a prelude to whatever news item is next on the agenda. Through the technological breakthrough of genetic forensics (or perhaps he said forensic genetics), cold case investigators in Bakersfield, California, had determined the identity of the alleged perpetrator of a rape and murder that took place half a century ago.

We were on the living room sofa, all four of us. TiVo had been silently recording the NBC *Nightly News* while we finished dinner, and with the table cleared and the plates loaded in the dishwasher, we'd sat down to watch it as we did more nights than not. It never takes much more than twenty minutes of our time, as we can speed through commercials; even so, Kristin's rarely there for more than half of it.

She was still sitting next to her mother tonight when they showed the photos, the original and the new improved version, individually at first, then side by side. We also got to see what's probably the only extant photo of Cindy Raschmann, one I recognized not because it resembled my memory of her but because I'd seen it in earlier coverage of the case.

They gave the name of the man, whom they were careful to call the *alleged* killer. He was Roger E. Borden, and he'd evidently disappeared without a trace after having left home not long after his high school graduation, several years before the rape and murder of Ms. Raschmann. Where he'd gone, what he'd done, and what had led him to Bakersfield seemed to be unknown, as did whatever course his life might have taken after the incident.

There was at present no way to know if Borden was alive or dead; if alive, he could be virtually anywhere, although almost all of the persons with whom he shared DNA seemed to be located west of the Rocky Mountains. But, NBC's breathless reporter on the scene stressed, this was very much an ongoing investigation, and authorities were optimistic that more information would be forthcoming. Meanwhile, there was an 800 number for viewers to call if they had information about Roger Borden's life before or after the murder. Or if they recognized the man in the photos, and had knowledge of where he might be living now.

We sat in silence, watching. They cut to a commercial, and it took a moment before Alden picked up the remote and hit the Fast Forward button. Kristin picked that moment to head off to her room, and once she was out of earshot someone could have said something, but no one did.

I didn't pay much attention to the rest of the newscast. My eyes saw what they showed on the screen, my ears took in what they had to say, but nothing really registered. I was waiting to see if they'd show the two photographs again, my long-ago yearbook photo and its aged version, but it wasn't that urgent an item, and once was enough.

Alden turned off the TV, and broke the silence that followed with his pronouncement: The man on the screen was no one he'd ever seen before.

I of course had recognized the yearbook photo immediately. I even remembered the sport jacket, and the tie. I'd only owned two or three ties, and rarely needed to wear one. The one in the photo, I seemed to remember, was striped in red and navy. But I wouldn't swear to that.

As for the older version, I don't know that it looked much like the face I see in the mirror every morning. But I recognized myself in it, perhaps because I could see the young Roger Borden staring back at me through the older Roger Borden's eyes.

But did it look like the man I'd become over the years?

Hard to say.

What I did say was that NBC had very likely given the item more attention than it would get on the other networks. A couple of years ago they'd included Cindy Raschmann's murder in a *Dateline* episode covering three cold cases. That didn't give them proprietary rights in the matter, but it had supplied them with clips and footage, along with an opportunity to plug *Dateline*.

"We may see those pictures again," I said. "Or we may not. It depends what response they get."

"Calls to that 800 number," Louella said.

"People who went to school with me, or think they did. People who saw me just last week at the Greyhound station in Spokane, or on a park bench in Oakland. People who can detect a resemblance between that picture and the grouchy neighbor they've never liked, and always wondered about."

" 'You rotten kids get off my lawn!' " Alden said.

"Ideally, they'll get a few dozen calls, all of them from the West Coast. And long before they've finished checking them all out, everyone will forget about tonight's news."

"That picture? Kristy didn't even look twice at it."

"No."

"She could have said, 'Hey, you know who that looks like?' The way you'd say the dog on *The Simpsons* was acting like Chester. But she didn't."

No, she hadn't.

"So maybe you looked like that once. But not anymore."

And so we reassured each other that there was nothing to worry about. And here I am at my desk, wondering if I believe it.

HARD TO SAY. Hard to know what to believe, and how anxious to be.

Just now, I opened the top center drawer of my desk. I was looking for the key that opens the locked drawer, and I found it readily enough, but didn't pick it up, didn't even touch it. All I did was look at it for a moment before I closed the drawer again.

To reassure myself that it was there? And that, by extension, the locked drawer was mine to open?

Maybe.

I always knew this could happen. I had hoped that it wouldn't, but had known all along that it might. I can't say I'd anticipated seeing my young self on the television screen, nor had I ever imagined a computer-aged version.

But I had relatives who'd submitted DNA, and when the right person looked in the right place, a match would turn up. And one thing would lead to another, and before too long they'd have the name of the brother who'd just plain vanished.

If *America's Most Wanted* were still on the air, its next episode would show those photos, and whatever else they could turn up. But the program went off the air a few years ago.

Well, they did have a run of almost twenty-five years. That's pretty good. And I've had an even longer run, haven't I?

I don't know where this goes. I can't rule out the possibility that someone right here in Lima will have seen something in those photographs. Someone who knows me from one of my clubs, someone who's seen me at the store. Or walking in the neighborhood, or standing in line at the grocery store.

Someone who knows only that there's something vaguely familiar about the guy in the picture. And then, a day or a week later, he catches a glimpse of me and the bell rings or the penny drops, however you want to put it, and it all comes together for him.

Should he pick up the phone, call the number? You don't want to get involved, and you certainly don't want to make trouble for an innocent man, but how often do you get a chance to solve a horrible crime and bring a vicious killer to justice? When you do, how can you shirk your responsibilities?

But of course you didn't bother to write down the 800 number, so maybe you should just let it go. If the connection's a real one, you can't be the only person who made it. Let someone else pick up the phone.

Still, how hard would it be to Google your way to the number?

And so on.

All I can do is wait. And that may not be easy, but neither will it be impossible, because God knows it's something I know how to do.

I've been waiting for all these years.

THREE WEEKS SINCE my last entry.

Not quite. It was nineteen days ago that Lester Holt showed my high school yearbook photo to his substantial and far-flung audience. It may have appeared elsewhere—on other network news broadcasts, on true-crime cable channels. The only newspaper I read regularly is the *Lima News*, and it would be bad news indeed if my picture showed up there, as that would only happen after I'd been arrested and charged.

I pick up the *New York Times* now and then, and *USA Today* once in a while, but I haven't seen either in the past three weeks. In fact I've made it a point not to look at them, or to check them out online. I'm sure the news item got attention in and around Bakersfield, and there'd surely be coverage in the local paper there at least as extensive as NBC's, but I don't feel the need to see it. And I doubt the Bakersfield *Californian* has many regular readers in western Ohio.

Easy enough to Google *Roger Borden* and see what shows up.

Easier still not to bother.

I did have the impulse, immediately after I got to see myself on NBC, to do what I could to make myself less visible. I could show up less frequently at the store, and spend more of my time there out of sight in the office in back. I could use the excuse of a bad back to skip a couple of bowling sessions; all of my teammates are apt to be sidelined now and then by

a backache or a troublesome knee or some other age-appro-
priate infirmity.

I could miss a few meetings of my clubs and civic groups,
and make fewer lunch dates. I could even invent a pretext—a
household retailers' convention, the funeral of an imaginary
relative—and leave town for a week or two.

There was some logic to all of that. Why put my face where
people might see it before time had given them a chance to
forget what they'd glimpsed on TV? Wasn't it better to keep
my exposure to a minimum?

I shared the notion with Louella, and she thought it over.
"Where would you go?" she wondered. "And what would you
do when you got there?"

"Some chain motel," I said. "At some Interstate exit in Indiana or Kentucky."

"In other words, out of state."

"I would think, though I'm not sure it would make any
difference. As far as what I'd do there, probably as little as
possible. Sit in my room, read a book, watch a movie on TV.
Go to the nearest diner for my meals."

"The same place every time?"

"Maybe not. Maybe I'd pick up fast food at a drive-through
window. Or order in."

"You might get tired of pizza."

"I'm tired already just thinking about it. You know what?
It's not a good idea."

"No."

"I'd be that guy who never leaves his room and has all his
meals delivered. Pays in cash, too, and what's that about? And

when I did go out, anybody who caught sight of me would see a stranger, and wonder if I looked familiar, and if they'd seen me anywhere before."

"While anybody who sees you at Thompson Dawes or the bowling alley would think *Oh, there's John.*"

" 'Good old John. Hell of a nice guy.' "

"They'd know right off who you were and wouldn't have to waste time thinking about you."

"And thinking about me," I said, "has always been a waste of time. But you're right. Better to be seen by people who don't have to wonder who it is they're looking at."

AND SO I'VE been living my life, doing what I've always done, going where I've always gone. It seems to me that the best way to draw unwanted attention is to make an effort to avoid it. Shrink into the shadows and people want to get a clearer view of you. Act as if you have something to hide and people can't help wondering what it might be.

This didn't mean that I had to overcompensate, shouldering my way into any spotlight, asserting my opinion in every conversation. The answer, I decided, lay somewhere in the middle: "Just be yourself."

Whoever that might be.

IT FEELS STRANGE.

It's been almost a full year since the last entry. I rarely go more than a few days between visits to my home office, and I generally boot up the laptop and do what one does on one's computer. I cope with email, I visit some websites I find interesting, I even make occasional entries in a rudimentary daybook I've taken to keeping.

It's nothing like this document, where I've allowed myself to think out loud.

Well, not out loud, obviously. How to phrase it? To ruminate in print, or perhaps in pixels. To do my thinking on screen.

I jot things down, keep certain records. My weight, on which my doctor wants me to keep an eye. My blood pressure, for which I now take a pill every morning.

The same annual physical which occasioned these measures led Alden and Kristin to buy me a birthday present, a wristwatch I'm to wear 24/7, except when I take it off to recharge it. It tells me far more than the time, monitoring my heartbeat and keeping track of my physical activity.

If the device had its way, I'd take upwards of ten thousand steps every day. That would presumably make my physician happy, even as it would lead to my wearing out my shoes faster, but I'm not all that certain it would have a discernible effect on either my weight or my blood pressure. There are days when I log ten thousand steps, and there are days when I don't, and I don't get all that worked up about it one way or the other.

Still, one has to pay a certain amount of attention to the

damned thing. I'll look at it, and see that I'm less than a thousand steps short of my daily goal, and as often as not I'll grab
the leash and whistle up Chester for a walk around the block.
Sometimes, of course, I'll say the hell with it and make myself
a sandwich instead, but all in all our faithful Rottweiler gets
more exercise than he used to, and so, I must admit, do I.

And if I remember, I log the day's step count in my daybook, along with my weight and blood pressure and anything
else I feel like keeping track of.

Bowling scores. Books I'm reading.

Odds and ends.

THE DAYBOOK'S A habit I got into without much thought,
and it's only now that I can see I can't attribute it solely to my
birthday present. Now that I've opened up this file, which began with my recalling significant chunks of my past and led to
my recording day-to-day developments, I realize how much a
part of my life it had become.

It was the place where I could tell myself what I'd never
told myself before, a place for all those matters I couldn't
mention to anyone else. I was selective, I'd run sentences
through my mind before I wrote them out, but most of what
went on inside me wound up on the computer screen in one
form or another.

And even when I elected not to jot something down, or
did so only to delete it, it got more of my attention than it

would otherwise have received. At this desk, on this computer, with my eyes on the screen and my fingers poised above the keyboard, I had no choice but to look at myself and my life a little differently.

I guess that's obvious.

Maybe it's time for me to read what I've written. All of it, top to bottom.

SO I'M HERE, and after typing the last sentence I sat down and read the last entry from a year ago, and then I scrolled all the way up to the very beginning of the file and read through everything that preceded it. All of it, all the way from *A man walks into a bar* to *Just be yourself, whoever that might be.*

A curious experience. There were sections I could almost take in at a glance, so familiar to me, so much a part of my consciousness, that I could probably have reproduced them word for word. And there were other passages I could only barely recall, as if I'd come across them in a dream.

I'm struck by how the tone has changed over time. It's as if several different men have shared the task of narration. At first we hear Buddy, and somewhere along the way he passes the microphone to Mr. Thompson. And now it's in the hands of Old Man Thompson, still reasonably hale and hearty but mellowed and rendered more pensive by the passing years.

And still a free man. There were indeed a handful of people who'd thought they recognized the two photographs of

Roger Borden, one as he once was, the other as he might have grown to be. In a few instances the recognition was real enough; they'd gone to school with Roger, or remembered him from the neighborhood. That was enough to get them to call the 800 number, but it didn't give them anything useful to report. *Yes, I remember Roger. The last person you'd figure would do something like that.* Or, just as likely: *That's Roger, all right. You know, there was always something about him. So I can't say I'm surprised.*

Right.

Others must have been more promising, and in the long run more of a nuisance. They were from viewers who were fairly certain they recognized the man who was being sought, that he was assistant produce manager of a supermarket in Bend, Oregon, or a night clerk at a none-too-reputable motel outside of Boise, or their own next-door neighbor, who revealed his own dark nature when a neighborhood dog had an accident on his lawn.

And so on.

Promising, because those were the sort of leads the police could not ignore. And a nuisance because they never led anywhere.

Did anyone turn up who thought that the kid in the sport coat and striped tie, given a change of clothes, might have filled their gas tank back in the day? Did anybody remember seeing Buddy across a liquor-store counter, or grabbing a burger at Denny's?

If so, I never heard about it.

As far as I can make out, the long arm of the law never

reached over the Rockies, let alone across the Mississippi River or the Ohio state line. My guess is the state and local authorities congratulated themselves on having taken it as far as they had, and getting prime air time on a network newscast. The response let them feel good about their efforts, and they could even draw some measure of satisfaction from the essentially useless confirmation, furnished by my one-time schoolmates and neighbors, that the picture on the screen was indeed that of young Roger. They already knew that, but wouldn't it gladden their hearts all the same?

And I think I can guess the prevailing attitude once every lead had been shown to lead nowhere. If I were involved in the investigation, it seems to me I'd take note of a couple undeniable facts about Roger Borden. First of all, he'd committed what looked like a random and impulsive murder all those years ago—and had never been arrested since, for any infraction of the law.

All those years? A drifter, capable of homicide, never getting picked up and charged with anything?

I'd think about that, and I'd think about just how many years it had been, and how old he'd have to be now. Living the life he must have led, very likely abusing drugs and alcohol, capable of violence, ruled by his impulses, almost certainly a sociopath.

And another thing. All those years, and all those brothers and sisters, and he'd never been in touch with any of them? No drunken phone calls? No urgent appeals for cash, or a night's lodging? Nothing? They'd been in touch with everybody, every surviving relative, every classmate they could find, and not a single person had had a single word from him since he killed that girl.

Well, hell, do the math. The son of a bitch would have to be dead by now, wouldn't you say? I mean, what are the odds?

I'M SURE IT'S still an open case. And I'm sure the cable channels, with their apparently unquenchable appetite for true crime, will do what they can to keep Cindy Raschmann—and Roger Borden—from slipping entirely out of sight. But there's always someone with a new solution to the unknowable identity of Jack the Ripper, or freshly discovered positive proof as to the actual authorship of Shakespeare's plays. That's enough to draw a little media attention, but it never seems to amount to very much.

So it really does look as though I've gotten away with it.

This evening—and it's early morning at this point, closer to daybreak than to bedtime—this evening, as I was reading, I found myself wondering if anybody ever gets away with anything. Who I am, what I've become, the life I've led and am leading now, are all part of a direct progression that began when a man walked into a bar.

I've had, as it turns out, a rich and satisfying life. I'm sure it looks enviable from a distance—a fairly prosperous businessman, active in civic affairs, still in reasonably good health, a devoted husband and father genuinely loved by his wife and children.

Not a few men would look at me and wish they could trade places.

And it's at least as satisfying from my point of view. I never could have predicted anything like this for myself. I'd never have dreamed of it, wished for it, imagined it as attainable.

And I've so utterly grown into it that it seems the life I was born to lead.

BUT, LEST I forget, it could still all end tomorrow. Someone somewhere could be struck by a blinding flash of recognition. *By God, that photograph! You know who that has to be?*

And then a phone call.

That's always something that could happen, and it will continue to be a possibility for as long as I am alive. The moving finger writes, or doesn't write. And no one can say which it'll be.

And if it happens?

I'm sure the revolver's still in the locked drawer. And I'm at least as sure that it will remain there, no matter who shows up on our front porch. I can't say whether that would be the easy or the hard way out, but it's not one I'll choose.

For now, all I know is it's way past my bedtime, and I'd like to get a couple of hours of sleep before I get up to face another day.

Whatever happens, I have the feeling I'll be okay with it.

My Newsletter: I get out an email newsletter at unpredictable intervals, but rarely more often than every other week. I'll be happy to add you to the distribution list. A blank email to lawbloc@gmail.com with "newsletter" in the subject line will get you on the list, and a click of the "Unsubscribe" link will get you off it, should you ultimately decide you're happier without it.

LAWRENCE BLOCK is a Mystery Writers of America Grand Master. His work over the past half century has earned him multiple Edgar Allan Poe and Shamus awards, the U.K. Diamond Dagger for lifetime achievement, and recognition in Germany, France, Taiwan, and Japan. His latest novel is *Dead Girl Blues*; other recent fiction includes *A Time to Scatter Stones, Keller's Fedora*, and *The Burglar in Short Order*. In addition to novels and short fiction, he has written episodic television (*Tilt!*) and the Wong Kar-wai film, *My Blueberry Nights*.

Block contributed a fiction column in *Writer's Digest* for fourteen years, and has published several books for writers, including the classic *Telling Lies for Fun & Profit* and the updated and expanded *Writing the Novel from Plot to Print to Pixel*. His nonfiction has been collected in *The Crime of Our Lives* (about mystery fiction) and *Hunting Buffalo with Bent Nails* (about everything else). Most recently, his collection of columns about stamp collecting, *Generally Speaking*, has found a substantial audience throughout and far beyond the philatelic community.

Lawrence Block has lately found a new career as an anthologist (*At Home in the Dark; From Sea to Stormy Sea*) and holds the position of writer-in-residence at South Carolina's Newberry College. He is a modest and humble fellow, although you would never guess as much from this biographical note.

Email: lawbloc@gmail.com
Twitter: @LawrenceBlock
Facebook: lawrence.block
Website: lawrenceblock.com

CPSIA information can be obtained
at www.ICGtesting.com
Printed in the USA
LVHW082228140620
658041LV00012B/403